# KATIE KAZOO, SWITCHEROO

# A Katie Kazoo Christmas

by Nancy Krulik • illustrated by John & Wendy

Grosset & Dunlap

For the real Brigandi family—N.K.

To M.G. Brinkman, King of Toys—J&W

GROSSET & DUNLAP
Published by the Penguin Group
Penguin Group (USA) Inc., 375 Hudson Street, New York, New York 10014, U.S.A.
Penguin Group (Canada), 10 Alcorn Avenue, Toronto, Ontario, Canada M4V 3B2
(a division of Pearson Penguin Canada Inc.)
Penguin Books Ltd, 80 Strand, London WC2R 0RL, England
Penguin Ireland, 25 St Stephen's Green, Dublin 2, Ireland
(a division of Penguin Books Ltd)
Penguin Group (Australia), 250 Camberwell Road, Camberwell,
Victoria 3124, Australia
(a division of Pearson Australia Group Pty Ltd)
Penguin Books India Pvt Ltd, 11 Community Centre, Panchsheel Park,
New Delhi - 110 017, India
Penguin Group (NZ), Cnr Airborne and Rosedale Roads, Albany, Auckland 1310,
New Zealand
(a division of Pearson New Zealand Ltd)
Penguin Books (South Africa) (Pty) Ltd, 24 Sturdee Avenue, Rosebank,
Johannesburg 2196, South Africa

Penguin Books Ltd, Registered Offices:
80 Strand, London WC2R 0RL, England

Text copyright © 2005 by Nancy Krulik. Illustrations copyright © 2005
by John and Wendy. All rights reserved. Published by Grosset & Dunlap,
a division of Penguin Young Readers Group, 345 Hudson Street,
New York, New York 10014. GROSSET & DUNLAP is a trademark
of Penguin Group (USA) Inc. Printed in the U.S.A.

*Library of Congress Cataloging-in-Publication Data is available.*

ISBN 0-448-43970-0          10 9 8 7 6 5 4 3 2

# Table of Contents

# Lights Out!

# Chapter 1

"Watch me, Katie," Suzanne Lock told her best friend, Katie Carew. She stood in the center of her bedroom and kicked her right leg high in the air. Then she kicked up her left leg. "The dancers in the show all join arms and kick their legs like this. Right. Left. Right. Left!" Suzanne shouted.

"The Cherrydale Christmas Extravaganza sounds like a really cool show," Katie said as she watched Suzanne dance around the room.

"Oh, it is," Suzanne agreed. She flopped down on her bed and sighed. "At the end of the performance, white snowflakes fall from the ceiling of the arena. And then Santa rides onto the stage in his sleigh and waves to everyone."

"Wow!" Katie said. "I would *really* love to see that."

"I wish you could come with us this year," Suzanne agreed. "But you can't get a ticket now. The Christmas Extravaganza has been sold out for months."

"You mean you're going to see it *again*?" Katie asked, surprised.

Suzanne nodded. "My dad got tickets from someone at his office. This is the third year in a row we're going to the show," she boasted. "I never get tired of it."

Katie could understand that. The Cherrydale Christmas Extravaganza sounded amazing with all those snowflakes, dancers dressed in red and white costumes, and Santa Claus, too.

"Come on, let's do the dance together," Suzanne said. She jumped up and pushed her night table against the wall so there could be

more room for them to dance. "We c
our own Christmas Extravaganza."

"Well, I could try," Katie agreed.
linked her arm through Suzanne's and began
to kick her legs straight out.

*Right, left. Right, left,* she repeated over
and over to herself as she tried to move her
legs at the same time as Suzanne's.

"Christmas is here, time to cheer," Suzanne
sang as they danced. "It's a spectacular time
of year!"

✕  ✕  ✕

It was already getting dark by the time
Katie began walking home from Suzanne's
house. That was the problem with winter. It
got dark so early. Usually that made Katie
kind of angry.

But not this week. Nothing could make
Katie angry the week before Christmas!

As Katie turned the corner, she glanced
in the open windows of the houses on her
block. Most homes had Christmas trees set

, in their living rooms. Many of the houses had pretty, colorful lights on the roofs and around their windows. A few had pine-green Christmas wreaths on their doors. They were all very beautiful.

But every year, the most spectacular house on the block belonged to Mr. Brigandi. His house was always covered with lots and lots of decorations.

Mr. Brigandi lived two doors down from Katie. Every year he went crazy decorating his house for Christmas. And this year was no exception.

Christmas was still a few days away, but he had already placed a giant Santa on his roof. The Santa moved up and down, so it looked like he was going down the chimney and coming back up. A big sleigh, pulled by electric reindeer, sat on the roof right beside Santa.

Mr. Brigandi had also hung red and green lights in all of his trees. He'd placed angels and shimmery, silver snowflakes on the branches, between the lights.

The house looked terrific. There was no doubt in Katie's mind that Mr. Brigandi was going to win the block association's best-decorated-house contest . . . *again*. Mr. Brigandi had won the contest for the past five years. Nobody else had even come close.

*Until now.*

As Katie reached the next house on the block—the one right between her house and Mr. Brigandi's—she was met by an unbelievable surprise. That house was all lit up, too. It was covered in white lights. There was a jolly-looking plastic Santa on the porch, and candles in all the windows.

Best of all, in the middle of the front lawn, there was a small Ferris wheel—a working one that went around and around. Little dolls were perched in its seats. Each doll was dressed in a costume from a different country. The song "It's a Small, Small World" played over and over as the Ferris wheel turned. It was pretty incredible.

But even *more* incredible was the fact that this unbelievable winter wonderland was at Mrs. Derkman's house!

The *same* Mrs. Derkman who had been Katie's strict, grumpy third-grade teacher.

The *same* Mrs. Derkman who read notes out loud just to embarrass her students and who gave homework over vacations.

The *same* Mrs. Derkman who hardly ever smiled—unless she was singing to the plants in her garden.

It was really hard to believe that this beautiful house belonged to Mrs. Derkman. But it was true.

Katie grinned. Christmas really *was* the season for surprises!

# Chapter 2

On Saturday afternoon, the kids in Katie's cooking club gathered in the Carew family's kitchen. They were all very excited. This wasn't just any meeting of the cooking club. This week, the kids were baking holiday cookies!

"*Mmmm*. These are delicious," George Brennan said as he bit into a tree-shaped sugar cookie.

Suzanne made a face. "George, wait until you're finished chewing before you talk," she told him.

George opened his mouth wide, showing his half-chewed cookie.

"Ugh," Miriam Chan groaned, turning away from George. "That's so gross."

"These cookies are really yummy," Emma Weber said, trying to turn the attention away from George. "I can't wait to bring them home. My brothers and sister will love them!"

"My mom says I'm not allowed to bring any cookies home," Mandy Banks told her. "We have too many sweets in the house already."

"I know what you mean," Kevin Camilleri agreed. "My house is filled with candies and cookies. And of course, we have my Aunt Edna's fruitcake. We get one of those every year."

"I *hate* fruitcake," Suzanne said with a frown.

"So do I," Kevin agreed. "Everyone in my family does. We never eat Aunt Edna's cake. We always bring it to the homeless shelter on Christmas Eve. Then we help out by serving dinner there."

"I bet the people there don't like your Aunt

Edna's fruitcake, either," George teased.

"I think it's nice that Kevin's family takes food to the shelter," Emma W. said.

"So do I," Katie agreed. "In fact, I have a great idea!"

Jeremy Fox smiled. He loved Katie's great ideas. "What do you want to do, Katie?" he asked.

"I think we should make a whole lot of cookies," Katie said.

"We're already doing that, Katie Kazoo," George said, using the cool nickname he'd given Katie back in third grade.

"No, we have to make more. *Lots* more," Katie explained. "Then we can wrap them up like presents and take them to the homeless shelter for its holiday party. I know the people there would love them as much as we do!"

"That *is* a great idea, Katie," Jeremy agreed.

"Maybe we could help serve food at the holiday party, too," Emma W. suggested.

"It's really lots of fun," Kevin told her.

"Ruff! Ruff!" Katie's dog, Pepper, barked. He leaped up and put his paws on the kitchen counter. Then he reached his mouth up and tried to eat a cookie.

"No way, Pepper," Katie said with a laugh. She moved the plate of cookies out of his reach. "These are for the people at the shelter. I'll get you one of *your* cookies."

She reached into a cupboard and pulled out a dog treat. She tossed it high in the air. Pepper leaped up and caught the treat in his mouth.

"Good boy," Katie said. She patted him on the head. Then she turned to her friends. "Okay, so it's settled. We'll all meet here on Christmas Eve to watch the Christmas house-decorating contest. After they pick a winner, we'll go over to the shelter together."

"I'll have to ask my mom since it's Christmas Eve," George said. "We usually spend that night together as a family. But I'll bet she'd let me go serve food at the shelter for a little while."

"I know my parents will say it's okay," Emma W. said. "They'll probably even come and help."

"Why do we have to do this on Christmas Eve?" Suzanne demanded.

"Because that's the night they choose a winner in the house-decorating contest. And it's also the night the shelter has its big party," Katie explained.

"But *I* can't go on Christmas Eve," Suzanne said. "I'm going to the Cherrydale

Christmas Extravaganza that night."

"That's okay," Jeremy told her. "There are plenty of us. We won't even notice you're missing."

Suzanne stuck her tongue out at Jeremy. He stuck his tongue out at her.

Katie sighed. Jeremy and Suzanne were both her best friends. But they didn't like each other very much. "Come on, you guys," Katie said, trying to calm them down.

But Suzanne was too mad to calm down. "If you are going to give the cookies away without me, then *I'm* not going to help bake them," she declared. She threw her mixing spoon down on the counter and stormed out of the kitchen. A few seconds later, the kids heard the front door of the house slam behind her.

"Suzanne just doesn't have the holiday spirit," Jeremy said with a shrug as he bit down on a star-shaped cookie.

✕　✕　✕

After Katie's friends left, she helped her mother clean up the kitchen.

"I'm going to take Pepper out for a walk, okay, Mom?" Katie asked when they were done.

"Sure, honey," her mom replied.

Katie put on her coat, put Pepper on his leash, and walked outside.

Katie gasped. Clearly Mr. Brigandi had been really busy!

Now there were even more decorations on his lawn than ever before. Katie looked up at the giant wooden nutcracker right at the edge of Mr. Brigandi's walkway. It stood tall and straight, like it was guarding the house.

Beside the nutcracker stood a beautiful ballerina statue. It wore a pink tutu and had a silver crown on its head. Katie could hear the ballerina's motor purring as the statue turned around and around on its wooden toe shoe.

Obviously Mr. Brigandi wasn't giving up his first-place title without a fight!

Mr. and Mrs. Derkman seemed as determined as Mr. Brigandi to win the house-decorating contest. They'd added a giant Frosty the Snowman to their Christmas display. They had also sprinkled fake snow all over their lawn to make it look extra festive. And there were so many bright lights on their trees that it looked like the sun was shining all around their house.

"This is the most beautiful block in the whole world!" Katie shouted.

# Chapter 3

On Sunday morning, Katie woke up early and got dressed. She wanted to go to the mall with her mother. Mrs. Carew was the manager of the Book Nook bookstore in the Cherrydale Mall.

Usually, Katie's mother gave Katie money to spend when she went to the mall. But today, Katie was carrying her own money in her pocketbook. She'd been saving it up all year. She had $17.45! She was going to use the money to buy gifts for her parents and Pepper.

"Hello, Katie," Mr. Krasner, the owner of the Pet Stop, greeted her. "I'll bet you're here to buy a present for Pepper," Mr. Krasner said.

Katie nodded. "I want to be sure he has a gift to open on Christmas morning. It's not fair for him to be left out."

"I have just the thing for him," Mr. Krasner told her. He held up a red and white candy-cane-shaped toy. "This is a great chew toy. It even smells like peppermint. And you know how dogs like mint!"

Katie sniffed at the toy. "Yum," she said. "It's perfect! Pepper will love it!"

Mr. Krasner walked over to the counter with Katie. He put the candy cane in a bag. Then he added a few dog treats to the bag, too. "The candy cane costs $2.25," he told Katie. "The treats are on the house. They're my present to Pepper."

"Thank you," Katie said as she handed him two one-dollar bills and a quarter. "And Pepper says, 'thank you,' too."

Mr. Krasner laughed. "Tell him I said, 'you're welcome.'" He winked at Katie.

Katie smiled and took her bag.

"Wait a minute," Mr. Krasner said as Katie walked away. "Aren't you going to go to the back of the store and visit the guinea pigs and hamsters? Their cages are decorated with green and red chew sticks. I thought it would put them in the Christmas mood."

"I'll have to visit them another day," Katie told Mr. Krasner. "I have a lot of shopping left to do."

"Okay," Mr. Krasner said. "Have a great holiday!"

"You too!" Katie said. "Bye!"

Katie smiled as she left the store and walked around the mall. She couldn't wait for Christmas to come. But first, she had to finish her shopping!

# Chapter 4

Katie wasn't the only Cherrydale Elementary School fourth-grader shopping that afternoon. Katie soon spotted Suzanne and her mother standing outside a kids' clothing store. They seemed to be arguing.

"But I don't have that sweater in *pink*," Katie heard Suzanne tell her mother.

"Your red one is just fine," Mrs. Lock answered.

"Mom, you don't understand," Suzanne moaned. She turned slightly and noticed Katie standing there. "Tell her, Katie. Tell her how badly I need this pink sweater." She pointed to a fuzzy, pink turtleneck sweater in

the window of the shop.

"It's the same as your red one," Katie said.

Suzanne frowned. "Whose side are you on?" she demanded.

"I . . . well . . . I mean," Katie stammered, not knowing what to say. She didn't want to get in the middle of a fight between Suzanne and her mom.

"Suzanne, I'm tired," Mrs. Lock said. "I'm going to get a cup of coffee and sit for a few minutes.

"Why don't you and Katie go shopping for a little while? I'll meet you later."

"Fine." Suzanne reached into her pocketbook and pulled out a sheet of notebook paper. Both sides were completely covered with words. "Here," she said, handing the paper to her mom. "This is my Christmas wish list. Just in case."

Mrs. Lock smiled weakly. "Thank you for your help, dear," she said. "Now run along."

✕   ✕   ✕

"So what's on your wish list?" Suzanne asked Katie as they wandered off together.

Katie shook her head. *Wish list*? No way! Katie didn't make wishes anymore! She knew too much about what happened when wishes came true.

It all started when Katie had been in third grade. She'd had a really awful day. She'd lost the game for her football team, ruined her new pants, and burped in front of the whole class.

That night, Katie had wished she could be anyone else but Katie Carew. There must have been a shooting star overhead or something when she made that wish, because the next day, the magic wind came.

The magic wind was a wild, forceful tornado that circled around only Katie. The magic wind was so powerful that every time it came, it turned Katie into somebody else! Switcheroo!

The first time the magic wind came, it turned her into Speedy, her third-grade class's hamster. She'd spent the morning gnawing on chew sticks and trying to escape from Speedy's cage.

But that had been better than the time she'd turned into Lucille the lunch lady and had to spend the whole day dishing out stinky food to kids in the cafeteria. And she had started a food fight and almost gotten Lucille fired.

Another time the wind turned Katie into mean old Mrs. Derkman. That had been awful. Katie didn't want to be strict with her friends. But when she was nice, they wouldn't even listen to her. Katie was amazed. She had no idea Mrs. Derkman's job was so hard.

And then there was the time she'd turned into T-Jon, one of the singers in her favorite band, the Bayside Boys. She'd made such a mess of things that time, the band had almost broken up.

In fact, any time Katie turned into someone else, she caused them—and herself—a whole lot of trouble. That was why Katie didn't make wishes anymore. Wishes were dangerous.

"I don't have a Christmas list," she told Suzanne finally. "My parents usually get me great stuff without my having to ask for any-thing."

"You're lucky," Suzanne told her. "My parents need all the help they can get."

# Chapter 5

"I'm hungry," Katie said after she and Suzanne had been shopping for a while. Katie was carrying two bags. One had Pepper's present in it. The other held a little toy roller coaster. Katie had bought that for her grandma. Katie's grandmother loved roller coasters. "You want to go to the food court?" she suggested.

Suzanne grinned. "I have an idea. How about we get something at Cinnamon's Candy Shop?"

"Ooh, yummy!" Katie squealed. "I love her gingerbread!"

"I can't believe my mom didn't want me to

have that pink sweater," Suzanne moaned as the girls turned and headed toward the candy store. "It would have been the perfect thing to wear to the Christmas Extravaganza." She looked at Katie. "You're so lucky. It doesn't matter what *you* wear Christmas Eve. You're just going to put an apron over it anyway when you serve food at the shelter. But I have to look good. So many people will be seeing my outfit."

Katie frowned. It wasn't like Suzanne was going to be onstage at the Extravaganza. No one was going to be looking at her. "Suzanne, you don't have any Christmas spirit," Katie told her.

"How can you say that?" Suzanne demanded. She pointed to her reindeer-shaped earrings. "See. I do too have spirit."

"Christmas isn't just about reindeer and Santa Claus and presents, you know," Katie insisted. "It's about being nice, and helping people, and . . ."

"Sure, sure, sure," Suzanne interrupted. "But everybody likes presents. And you have to admit that it's fun seeing all the pretty lights and decorations."

Katie didn't know what to say. Suzanne was right. She did like presents and lights. But that didn't make the way Suzanne had been acting any better.

"Look, even Mrs. Derkman agrees with me," Suzanne continued. She pointed toward the hardware store. At that very moment, the teacher was walking out of the shop with a pile of Christmas lights in her arms. Mr. Derkman followed behind her, carrying a family of plastic elves.

"Hello," Mrs. Derkman called out to the girls.

"Hello, Mrs. Derkman," Katie said.

"Wow, look at all those lights!" Suzanne exclaimed. "Your house is going to be the most beautiful in the whole neighborhood."

"That's the idea," Mrs. Derkman said. "In

our old neighborhood, we were the only house that put up lots of decorations." She stopped for a minute and sighed. "Of course, that's different now."

"You mean Mr. Brigandi's house?" Katie said.

"Yes," Mrs. Derkman said. "Although I think his decorations are so tacky. Ours are much more tasteful."

Katie looked at the bright red and green elves Mr. Derkman was carrying in his arms. They looked kind of tacky, too.

"I noticed that your parents put up very few lights," Mrs. Derkman mentioned to Katie.

"We always decorate our house the same way," Katie said. "Blue and white lights on our trees and around our window sills."

"Very traditional," Mrs. Derkman replied. "But maybe you'd all like to try something new this year. I'd be glad to give your parents some lessons on the fine art of Christmas decorating."

Decorating lessons? Somehow Katie couldn't imagine her parents taking lessons on how to decorate. She wondered if Mrs. Derkman would make them write a term paper on the proper way to hang a wreath or something.

"I think they like our house the way it is," Katie said.

"I'm just letting you know I'm here if you want some help," Mrs. Derkman replied.

"Uh, Snookums?" Mr. Derkman interrupted.

"Yes, Freddy Bear?" Mrs. Derkman replied.

Katie tried hard not to laugh. The Derkmans' pet names for each other were *so* mushy.

"These elves are getting very heavy. I think we need to head to the parking lot," Mr. Derkman said.

"Okay, dear. Let's go." Mrs. Derkman looked at the girls. "I'll see you both tomorrow night. It's Christmas Eve, the night of the big contest."

"I won't be there," Suzanne told her. "I'm going to the Cherrydale Christmas Extravaganza."

"Sorry you'll miss all the fun," Mrs. Derkman said. "You'll have to come by and see our trophy one day."

Katie sighed. Mrs. Derkman was so certain she would win the contest. Maybe she shouldn't be so confident. After all, she had some pretty stiff competition at Mr. Brigandi's house.

# Chapter 6

"Come on, Katie," Suzanne said as soon as the Derkmans had gone. "Let's get going to Cinnamon's. I can't wait to try the gingerbread!"

Katie followed Suzanne into the store.

"Hi, girls," Cinnamon said, greeting Katie and Suzanne as they came through the door. The candy-store owner was dressed in a red dress with white trim. She had on a red-and-white Santa hat.

"Hi, Cinnamon," Katie answered.

"Have you girls come in for a treat?" Cinnamon asked.

"Of course," Suzanne replied. "Do you

have any more of your home-baked ginger-bread cookies? We really love them."

"I think there may be a few in the back," Cinnamon said. "Let me go check."

As Cinnamon went into the back room to look for the cookies, Katie and Suzanne wandered around the store. Cinnamon's Candy Shop always smelled good. But this year it smelled doubly delicious. Katie took a deep breath. The sweet scent of chocolate mixed in the air with nutmeg, gingerbread, cinnamon, and minty candy canes.

"I love it in here," Katie said. "It smells just like Christmas."

Just then, a tall man with gray hair popped out from behind the candy canes. "I know what you mean," he told Katie. "I wish I could bottle this smell and cover my whole house with it."

Katie grinned. "Hi, Mr. Brigandi."

"Hi, girls," Mr. Brigandi replied.

"Your house looks really pretty this year,"
Suzanne told him. "You have a lot of extra
lights and new decorations."

"I thought it was time to make some
changes," Mr. Brigandi replied. "*Especially*
with the new competition on the block."

"The Derkmans' house is pretty
incredible," Suzanne agreed. "They'll be
tough to beat."

"Oh, I'll win the contest," Mr. Brigandi
assured her. "I always do."

"Mrs. Derkman thinks *she's* going to win,"
Katie told him. "She's working hard on her
decorations. I just saw her buying a whole
bunch of Christmas lights at the hardware
store."

"The Derkmans are buying *more* lights?"
Mr. Brigandi asked curiously. He shoved his
hands into the pockets of his dark blue jacket.

"Oh yeah," Suzanne said. "And little

plastic elves, too. We saw them."

Mr. Brigandi's face turned beet red. He frowned. "Elves, huh?" he harrumphed. "They think they can beat *me* with a bunch of elves? Ha! They've got another thing coming!"

"I didn't say they were going to beat you," Katie assured him. "I just meant that they want to win, too."

Mr. Brigandi handed Katie the candy cane he was holding. "I've got to run," he said as he dashed out of the store.

"I wonder where *he's* going in such a hurry," Suzanne said as she went over to look at some Christmas-tree-shaped chocolates.

"Probably to get more decorations for his house," Katie replied. "Did you see how angry he got when he heard the Derkmans had bought those elves?"

"I bet when the Derkmans see what Mr. Brigandi does at his house, they'll go out and buy more decorations, too," Suzanne said.

"And then Mr. Brigandi will buy more, just

so his house can have more decorations than the Derkmans' house," Katie added.

"And then the Derkmans will buy more . . ." Suzanne began.

"Grown-ups can be such babies sometimes!" Katie declared.

# Chapter 7

"This traffic is terrible!" Katie's mom groaned as she drove home from the mall that evening. "We haven't moved in fifteen minutes."

Katie looked out the window. There were cars for as far as she could see. That was very strange. Usually the trip from the mall took only ten minutes. But they'd already been in the car for almost half an hour.

Katie felt bad for her mom, who had been working so hard all day. She just wanted to go home and put up her feet. But she was stuck in traffic instead.

"I know how to cheer you up," Katie told her. She began to sing. "Deck the halls with boughs of holly, fa la la la la la la la la."

Mrs. Carew loved Christmas carols. She couldn't resist singing along. "'Tis the season to be jolly," she chimed in. "Fa la la la la la la la la."

Katie and her mom kept singing their favorite carols. It was a good thing they knew

a lot of them. They sang "The Twelve Days of Christmas" as well as "Jingle Bells," "Deck the Halls," and "The Little Drummer Boy" before they finally turned the corner onto their own street.

"Oh my goodness! Look at this," Mrs. Carew exclaimed. "All this traffic was coming from our block!"

It was true. There were a lot of cars driving down their street. Crowds of people were walking on the sidewalks. Many of those people had cameras. They were taking pictures of Mr. Brigandi's house and the Derkmans' house.

"We have *tourists* on our block," Katie said, amazed. She remembered what it was like to be a tourist. After all, she'd been one during her European vacation. But she'd taken pictures of palaces, churches, and art museums. She hadn't taken photos of people's homes. "This is so weird," she added.

There were so many people standing outside the Derkmans' house that Mrs. Carew had to honk her horn several times to get them to move away from the driveway so she could pull her car in.

Mrs. Carew scrambled out of the car. "Let's just get inside," she said, hurrying into the house. Katie followed close behind her mother.

"Arooo. Arooo." Katie heard Pepper's cries the minute her mother opened the door.

"Pepper, what's wrong?" Katie asked. She bent down and petted his little head.

"Ruff! Ruff!" the chocolate-and-white cocker spaniel barked.

"He's been barking ever since the Christmas lights went on next door," Katie's father said. "He's not happy about all the strangers in the neighborhood."

"I think he's trying to protect the house," Katie told her father. "That's his job." She smiled at Pepper. "You're a good boy," she told him.

Pepper rubbed up against Katie and wagged his brown, stubby tail.

"These crowds are really loud," Mrs. Carew said. "This whole Christmas decorating thing is getting out of hand."

"I know," Katie's dad agreed. "First the Derkmans put up those elves. Then Pete Brigandi came home and built a maze of giant plastic candy canes on his lawn. He's letting kids walk through the maze. It's brought people from all over the place to our block."

Katie frowned. She felt kind of responsible for that. If she and Suzanne hadn't told Mr. Brigandi about the Derkmans' new decorations, he never would have built the candy-cane maze.

"If these people don't go home soon, we won't get any sleep," Mrs. Carew said. "Tomorrow is Christmas Eve. The store is going to be very busy with last-minute shoppers. I need my rest."

"Aroo!" Pepper barked in agreement. "Ruff!"

Katie sighed. Christmas was supposed to be a time for peace on Earth. But there wasn't any peace on Katie's block tonight!

# Chapter 8

The smell of Christmas cookies filled the
air in Katie's house on Christmas Eve. All the
kids in Katie's cooking club were gathered
there, baking cookies and then wrapping them
in pretty green or red cling wrap.

"George, stop eating all the cookies,"
Miriam Chan said.

George shook his head. "You can get rich
by eating snacks, you know," he told her.

"How?" Miriam demanded.

"By eating fortune cookies!" George joked.
He laughed. Everyone else laughed, too.

"Well, these aren't fortune cookies," Katie
said. "And Miriam's right. We need all the

cookies we can get for the kids at the shelter."

"All right, I'll stop eating and start wrapping," George agreed, wiping a crumb from his mouth.

"Okay, everyone, here comes another batch of cookies, fresh out of the oven," Mr. Carew said. He placed the baking sheet on the counter.

Katie laughed. Her dad was wearing her mother's apron. It was pink and green. On the front it said, "Kiss the Cook."

"You look funny, Daddy," Katie giggled.

"Yeah, that apron is definitely not your style, Mr. Carew," Emma W. laughed.

"You don't think so?" Mr. Carew teased. He spun around like a model on a runway. "I think I'm making a fashion statement."

"It's a good thing Suzanne isn't here," Kevin told him. "She'd definitely have a few statements to make about your fashion."

Katie frowned when Kevin mentioned Suzanne. She missed having her at the

cooking club meeting. It wasn't as much fun without her.

"I can't imagine what happened to your mother," Mr. Carew wondered aloud. "I thought she'd be home to help by now."

"She probably got stuck in traffic again," Katie said.

"I hope she makes it home in time for the contest judging," Mr. Carew said. "I think Pete Brigandi has some real competition this year."

"I'll say," George agreed. "Who knew Mrs. *Jerk*man would be so into Christmas. When she was our teacher, she never let us do anything fun."

Katie frowned. Even though Mrs. Derkman wasn't their teacher anymore, it was obvious George still didn't like her. Not that Katie blamed him. Mrs. Derkman *had* been kind of mean to George.

"Who judges this contest?" Jeremy asked.

"It's always two people from our block

association," Katie explained.

"This year it's Sam Hanson and Sonia Diaz," Mr. Carew told the kids.

"What if they pick their own houses as the winners?" George asked suspiciously.

Mr. Carew shook his head. "The judges aren't allowed to win the contest. We keep everything fair and square around here."

"Except the cookies," Katie giggled. "They're round, not square."

"And they're tasty, too!" George said, reaching for another cookie.

"GEORGE!" the kids all shouted at once.

A few minutes later, Mrs. Carew came bursting through the front door. She had a big frown on her face. "I have had it!" she shouted angrily. "The traffic on this street is out of control!"

Pepper raced out of the kitchen to greet her. Mr. Carew followed close behind. At the sight of her husband, Mrs. Carew began to laugh. "Oh, you look so funny!" she giggled, pointing to the apron.

"Everyone's a fashion critic," Katie's dad said. But he wasn't angry. He was just glad he could make his wife smile.

Katie's parents walked back toward the kitchen together. "*Mmm*. It smells yummy in here," Mrs. Carew said, complimenting the kids.

"We're almost finished wrapping the cookies," Katie told her mom. "We'll be ready to go over to the shelter right after the contest."

"I can't wait for that Christmas contest to be over," Mrs. Carew said with a sigh.

"I thought you liked Christmas decorations," Jeremy said.

"I do," Mrs. Carew assured him. "But this year's contest is too much. You won't believe what's going on out there. There are about a hundred people. There's even a news van!"

Katie gasped. A news van! Everyone raced for the door, with Pepper barking at their heels.

# Chapter 9

"Wow!" Katie gasped as she stepped out of the house and onto her front lawn. "Look at all this."

Katie lived on a quiet little block in a quiet little town. But looking around, she could be in New York City. That's how crowded her street was. There were people everywhere!

"Yikes!" Jeremy exclaimed.

"I've never seen this many people in one place before," Emma W. said. "It looks like all of Cherrydale is here."

Kids were standing in front of Mr. Brigandi's and Mrs. Derkman's houses, taking pictures of one another with the decorations.

Dads lifted little kids onto their shoulders so the kids could see better over the crowds.

Cars moved through the streets. Drivers honked their horns as the traffic grew thicker and thicker.

News reporters stood by with their microphones in hand. Everyone seemed to be talking and pointing at once.

Katie and her parents didn't like the crowds, but the Derkmans sure seemed to. They were standing outside their house, proudly pointing out their decorations.

Katie looked over to see if Mr. Brigandi was doing the same thing. But Mr. Brigandi wasn't on his front lawn. In fact, he was nowhere near the crowds. Instead, he was on his roof, putting a few last-minute decorations on his house. Katie could see him up there, arranging more lights.

"Excuse me," a woman with two little girls said to Katie. "Could you move out of the way? I'm trying to get a picture of that house."

She pointed toward the Derkmans' home.

Pepper didn't like having strangers on his lawn. "Aroo!" he howled.

"Wah! Wah!" One of the little girls began to cry. "No like doggie."

"Could you stop that dog from barking at my children?" the woman demanded.

Katie couldn't believe what she was hearing. It was her front lawn, after all. "But . . ."

"Why don't you take Pepper back into the house?" Katie's mom cut in. "He can get hurt out here."

That was true. Katie hadn't looked at it that way. A little cocker spaniel could get trampled with all these people around. Katie quickly scooped up her dog in her arms and carried him back inside.

As soon as they were in the house, Pepper jumped up onto the couch and buried his little brown-and-white head in his paws. "Aroo," he whimpered.

"It's okay, boy," Katie said as she patted his

head. "They'll be gone soon."

Just then, Katie felt a light breeze blowing on the back of her neck. She turned to see if she'd left the door open. No. It was shut tight. The breeze was obviously not coming from the outside.

*Uh-oh!* That could mean only one thing. This was no ordinary breeze. This was the magic wind. It was back!

Katie gulped. Oh, no. Not now. Not on Christmas Eve!

But the magic wind didn't care about holidays. It came whenever it wanted to. And right now it was circling wildly around Katie. She shut her eyes tightly and tried not to cry.

The magic wind was really powerful tonight. It whirled faster and faster. It swirled like a horrible tornado. *A tornado that was blowing around only Katie.*

And then it stopped. Just like that.

The magic wind was gone.

And so was Katie Carew.

# Chapter 10

*Brrrr.* Katie shivered. She wasn't quite sure
where the magic wind had blown her. But
wherever it was, it was outside. And it was
cold!

Slowly, Katie opened her eyes and looked
around. She looked up. She looked down.

Uh-oh. Looking down had been a bad idea.
The magic wind had blown Katie all the way
to the roof of a two-story house! Down was
very far away! Katie was scared!

"AAAAAHHHHH!!" she screamed. But her
voice didn't sound like a fourth-grade girl's
scream. It had been a low, deep scream. A
*man's* scream.

Katie looked at herself. Her big brown boots were definitely men's shoes.

Her slacks were men's work pants.

Her hands were big and blistery. And they were covered with hair. Yuck!

But it was her coat that helped Katie figure out who she was. It was a dark blue jacket with a zipper up the front and pockets on the sides. Katie had seen Mr. Brigandi wear it lots of times.

Which could mean only one thing. Katie had been switcherooed into Mr. Brigandi . . . while he was standing all the way up there on his roof!

This was *so* not good!

Katie did not like being so far from the ground. She really wanted to be back down with everybody else. Quickly, she looked around for some way to get down. But she didn't see a ladder anywhere. There was no way for her to get off the roof. At least not that she could see.

There was also no way the magic wind
was going to come and change her back any-
time soon. Not with all those people down
there staring at her. The magic wind came
only when Katie was alone. And those people
weren't going to leave until after the contest
was over.

Which meant Mr. Brigandi wasn't going

to be around to see if he'd actually won. That seemed very unfair to Katie. After all, Mr. Brigandi had worked very hard to make his house look so special.

At least it seemed special from down below. Katie looked around. From up on the roof, the decorations weren't all that impressive. In fact, they looked kind of junky.

From close-up, it was obvious that the giant Santa was just a big chunk of painted plastic with a motor attached to its back. The motor whirred really loudly, making the Santa seem even *more* fake.

Not that Katie had ever thought that the Santa Claus was real or anything. But it had been fun to pretend.

Rudolph the red-nosed reindeer didn't look very nice from up close, either. His shiny nose was really just a big red lightbulb.

Katie bet the presents in the sleigh weren't real either. They were probably just empty boxes. She took a few steps toward the sleigh to get a better look, and . . .

*Whoa!* Katie tripped over a pile of Christmas lights that had been left on the roof.

"Oh, no!" Katie shouted. She grabbed on to the nearest thing she could find—the moving Santa Claus decoration.

The next thing she knew, Katie was sliding up and down as the Santa Claus moved in and out of the chimney on Mr. Brigandi's roof.

*Up. Down. Up. Down.*

"Ouch!" Katie cried.

"Hey, check out the guy on the roof!" Katie heard someone shout from down below.

"Yeah, he thinks he's Santa Claus!" someone else shouted. The crowd began to laugh.

Katie blushed. She was *so* embarrassed. Quickly, she let go of the Santa and scrambled to her feet.

"Okay, that wasn't so bad," she said to herself as she stood there for a moment. "I didn't fall off the roof or anything."

*At least not yet.*

# Chapter 11

It was getting colder up on the roof. Mr. Brigandi's jacket wasn't very warm. Katie shivered. She wanted to get inside.

But that meant getting off the roof somehow. And without a ladder, it seemed impossible.

Still, Katie figured the magic wind hadn't blown the real Mr. Brigandi up onto his roof. He must have climbed up *somehow*.

Katie walked carefully over toward one side of the house and looked down. There was an open window on the second floor. It led to one of the bedrooms. Mr. Brigandi must have climbed out the window to get to the roof.

*But how?* He would have needed a ladder to get from the window to the roof. And there wasn't one anywhere.

In fact, the only thing between the window and the roof of the house was a rose trellis. It was made of crisscrossed metal strips and attached to the side of the house. In the summer time, Mr. Brigandi's roses covered the frame. But in the winter, it was just thick strips of metal joined together.

*Sort of like a ladder.*

That was it! Mr. Brigandi must have climbed the trellis to reach the roof. And that was exactly how Katie was going to get down!

At least she thought that was how she'd do it. The truth was, that trellis looked scary. Mr. Brigandi never should have been climbing on it. Katie knew her mother would be angry if she knew Katie was climbing on it.

But it was the only way Katie was going to be able to get down. She would have to take a chance.

Slowly, Katie got on her knees and placed her foot on one of the metal strips. The trellis shook slightly, but it didn't fall.

"Okay, I can do this," Katie said to herself. "I just can't look down. That would be too scary."

Unfortunately, Katie *had* to look down to find the next strip in the trellis. And when she did, she realized just how high up she really was.

"Oh, no!" she gulped. Tears began to form in her eyes. This was the worst thing the magic wind had ever done to her.

She had to get inside that house! Katie carefully moved her foot down toward the next rung and . . .

Whoops! Her foot missed the metal strip.

"Aaaaaaaahhhhhh!" she cried out. Quickly, she grabbed hold of a metal box that was sticking out from the side of the house. She held on tight, until she could regain her footing.

As she placed her foot back on the trellis, Katie breathed a sigh of relief. "Everything's okay," she told herself quietly.

*Or not.*

At that very moment, everything went dark. Everything! The lights weren't flickering. The Santa wasn't moving up and down. And Rudolph no longer had a nose so bright.

"Hey, what happened?" Katie heard some of the people shout from below.

Katie figured out the answer to that one pretty quickly. That metal box must have been where all the decorations were plugged in. Katie must have disconnected the wires when she grabbed it.

Now Mr. Brigandi's house didn't look Christmassy at all. It just looked like a dark, empty house. And the judges were going to come by any minute.

Mr. Brigandi didn't have a chance of winning the contest now.

And it was all Katie's fault.

$$\times \quad \times \quad \times$$

Climbing down the trellis was doubly hard in the dark. But Katie kept going. She had to.

*Right foot, left foot, right foot, left foot,* she said over and over to herself as she moved slowly down the ladder

Finally, Katie managed to reach the open window. She scrambled into the house.

Yikes. It was really dark inside. The only light came from the moon. The trees outside were leaving weird shadows on the wall.

Katie shuddered. "This is the worst Christmas Eve ever!" she shouted into the darkness.

Suddenly, Katie felt a cold blast of wind hit her. It was like icy fingers crawling up her neck.

Katie pulled up the collar on Mr. Brigandi's coat to warm herself. But a coat was no match for this wind. This was the *magic* wind. And the magic wind was stronger than any jacket.

Within seconds, the breeze had turned into a full-force icy tornado that swirled and whirled around only Katie. She grabbed the bed and held on tight. She didn't want to wind up being blown back onto Mr. Brigandi's roof.

The wind grew colder and colder. It blew harder and harder.

And then it stopped. Just like that.

The magic wind was gone.

But Katie Carew was back.

# Chapter 12

Quickly, Katie darted down the stairs and out the front door. The crowd outside Mr. Brigandi's house was much smaller than it had been before. Most of the people had moved on to the Derkmans' house.

"Well, this house doesn't have a chance," Katie heard one boy say.

"I know," another boy replied. "Why would Mr. Brigandi turn out his lights just when the judges are coming by? How dumb is that?"

"I guess he didn't really want the trophy this year," the first boy answered.

Katie frowned. That wasn't true at all. Mr. Brigandi *had* wanted that prize. *Badly.* And she had ruined everything for him.

But Mr. Brigandi didn't know that. In fact, he was certain *someone else* had pulled the plug on his decorations.

"YOU!" Mr. Brigandi shouted as he ran across Katie's front lawn toward the Derkmans' house. "You did this to me!"

Mr. Derkman looked at him, surprised. "Did what?" he asked.

"You turned out my lights," Mr. Brigandi said accusingly.

"We did no such thing," Mrs. Derkman said.

"Yes you did. You were so desperate to win that you ruined my Christmas display," Mr. Brigandi shouted.

"How could we have done that?" Mr. Derkman demanded. "We've been standing here the whole time."

"I'm not sure how you did it," Mr. Brigandi admitted. He scratched his head. "I'm not really sure of anything right now. In fact, the last thing I really remember is being on my roof, putting the finishing touches on my decorations. The next thing I knew, I was on my front lawn, and the lights were out in my house. I don't even know how I got there."

"Well, maybe you turned off your own lights, then," Mrs. Derkman insisted, "because you knew we were going to win anyway. You just decided to surrender."

"Surrender? Me?" Mr. Brigandi shouted. "Never!"

The argument was getting really loud now. Everyone was screaming at once. Even the judges, Mr. Hanson and Mrs. Diaz, couldn't get a word in.

Katie couldn't believe it. Her neighbors had totally forgotten what Christmas was supposed to be about! It made her really angry.

"CUT IT OUT!" Katie shouted suddenly. "STOP IT!"

Mr. and Mrs. Derkman turned and stared at her.

So did Mr. Brigandi.

In fact, everyone stopped what they were doing to look at the redheaded fourth-grader who had yelled at her adult neighbors.

"What did you say?" Mrs. Derkman demanded. She sounded a lot like she had when she'd been Katie's third-grade teacher.

But Mrs. Derkman wasn't Katie's teacher anymore. She couldn't get her into any trouble here. "I said, 'Stop it!' " Katie repeated. "You guys are acting ridiculous."

"Katie!" Mrs. Carew scolded.

"No, Mom, it's true," Katie replied. "Christmas shouldn't be about contests. We shouldn't be thinking about who has the nicest lights, or who spent the most money on plastic elves and candy canes. We should be thinking about being nice to one another."

"You tell 'em, Katie Kazoo!" George shouted.

"While you grown-ups were busy decorating your houses, my friends and I were baking

74

cookies for the families at the shelter," Katie told them. "We were celebrating Christmas the right way."

"Woohoo!" The kids in the cooking club let out a huge cheer. "We rule!"

Mr. Derkman frowned and looked at the ground. Mrs. Derkman kicked at the fake snow below her feet.

"Katie's right," Mr. Brigandi said. "We were so focused on this contest, we forgot about

Christmas." He turned to Katie. "Would you kids like some grown-up help at the shelter tonight?"

"Definitely!" Katie told him. "I bet the kids in the shelter would love to have some Christmas lights in their windows."

Mr. Brigandi laughed. "I have a few of those they could borrow," he said. "And some big plastic candy canes, too."

"Elves would look nice at the shelter," Mr. Derkman suggested.

"And I think some of the little girls would like the dolls from our Ferris wheel," Mrs. Derkman added. "Dolls should be played with, not looked at."

Katie grinned. The grown-ups were acting like grown-ups again.

Finally.

# Chapter 13

"Wow! This place looks amazing!" Jeremy exclaimed as he looked around the shelter.

"It really does," Emma W. agreed. "The tree has so many lights on it!"

"And look at those kids going through the candy-cane-and-elf maze. They're having a blast," Miriam agreed. "Mr. Brigandi and Mr. Derkman sure put that together fast."

"Our cookies are a big hit," Kevin announced to everyone. "In fact, they're almost gone."

"The music is great," Katie said. "I love Christmas songs."

"I think Mrs. Derkman likes them, too,"

Jeremy said.

"Yeah, look at her go," George added.

Katie giggled. Her third-grade teacher was right in the middle of the dance floor. She and her husband were doing some weird, old-fashioned kind of dance. Mr. Derkman was pretending to swim. Mrs. Derkman was moving her hands up and down like a monkey, while her body jerked back and forth.

Mrs. Derkman could do a lot of things really well. But dancing sure wasn't one of them.

"What kind of dance is that?" Mandy asked, giggling.

"It's the *Jerk*man jerk," George joked.

The kids all started to laugh.

"Too bad Suzanne had to miss that," Mandy said as she watched Mrs. Derkman and her husband dance. "She would have loved to see Mrs. Derkman make a fool of herself."

"Hey, check it out," Jeremy shouted. He

pointed to the door. "There are news reporters here!"

Everybody's attention turned toward the
reporters and their cameras. They were busy
interviewing the kids who lived at the shelter.

"This is the best night of my whole life,"
one little boy said.

"Mine too," his sister told the reporter. She
held up a doll dressed in a lacy French dress.
"I got a dolly for Christmas. I never had such
a fancy dolly before."

That made Katie smile. Mrs. Derkman was
right. Dolls were meant to be played with.

"Let's talk to some of the kids who are vol-
unteering at the party," the reporter said. She
started over toward Katie and her friends.

But the reporter wasn't the only one trying
to get near the kids. Suzanne Lock was hurrying over toward them, too. And Suzanne was a
lot faster.

"Suzanne! You made it!" Katie shouted
excitedly. She gave her a big hug.

"Dad and I saw the first half of the show," Suzanne told her. "But the more I thought about it, the more I realized I wanted to be here with you."

"That's true," Mr. Lock said. "Suzanne and I were standing in the lobby at intermission. We heard some news reporters talking about coming down here to take pictures of the kids who were baking cookies for the shelter. She insisted we come here right away. She didn't want to miss out on all the fun."

Katie smiled. It was more likely that Suzanne didn't want to miss out on a chance at being on TV. In fact, Suzanne was already talking to the reporter.

"We have this cooking club," Suzanne told her. "And this week, we all decided to bake cookies for the shelter." She smiled brightly for the camera.

Katie sighed. Suzanne would probably be boasting about being on TV for weeks to come.

But that didn't matter. What mattered was that everyone was having fun together on Christmas Eve. Even Mrs. Derkman and Mr. Brigandi. They were doing the twist in the middle of the dance floor.

Katie smiled. Wow! Imagine Mr. Brigandi and Mrs. Derkman dancing together instead of arguing.

Now *that* was a switcheroo even the magic wind couldn't manage. It took *Christmas* magic to make that happen!

# That's a Wrap!

# Chapter 1

*Try Our Special Christmas Pizza!*

Katie Carew and Jeremy Fox stood outside Louie's Pizza Shop and read the sign in the window.

"*Christmas* pizza?" Jeremy asked. "What's that? Does he use green dough or something?"

Katie made a face. "*Ewww.* I hope not," she said.

"Well, there's only one way to find out," Jeremy said. He opened the door and walked into the restaurant. Katie followed close behind.

Katie was really hungry. She'd been

shopping for Christmas gifts all morning. So far, she'd bought only one present—a Christmas tree–shaped doggie toy. It was for her cocker spaniel, Pepper.

As Katie walked into the pizza place, she spotted her best friend Suzanne Lock. Suzanne was sitting at a table with Jessica Haynes, a girl from Suzanne's class. Katie's other friends, George Brennan, Kevin Camilleri, and Manny Gonzalez, were seated at the next table. Katie smiled. Louie's was the perfect place for kids to hang out while their parents shopped.

"Hi, Jeremy. Hey, Katie Kazoo!" George called, using the super-cool nickname he'd made up for Katie last year in third grade. "You're just in time. Louie's making a special Christmas pizza for us. Sit down."

"No way. Katie's sitting with *us*," Suzanne told George. "You guys can have Jeremy."

Katie and Jeremy looked at each other. They had been having fun together all day.

They didn't want to sit at different tables.

"How about we push these two tables together?" Katie suggested. "Then nobody has to split up."

"Whatever," Suzanne said with a shrug. But she didn't sound too happy about it.

"What's in the bag?" Jessica asked Katie.

"A Christmas present for Pepper," Katie told her. "I'm going to wrap it and put it under the tree for him. I don't want him to feel left out on Christmas morning."

"Katie, Pepper's a *dog*," Suzanne said with a laugh. "You don't have to wrap his gift. It's not like he'll know the difference."

"I'm going to wrap it," Katie insisted. "Pepper *will* notice. He knows a lot more than you think he does."

Nobody argued with her. There was no point. All of Katie's friends knew she thought Pepper was the smartest dog in the world.

"Pepper's really going to like that toy,"

Jeremy said, defending Katie. "Almost as much as I would like a snowboard for Hanukkah."

"Snowboards are so cool!" Kevin exclaimed. "Do you really think you're going to get one?"

"I sure hope so," Jeremy told him. "I've been wishing for one for a really long time."

"You'd better be careful what you wish for," Suzanne warned him. "Wishes don't always come true the way you think they will."

Katie gulped. She couldn't believe Suzanne had said that. Was it possible that she knew about the wish Katie had made—the one about being anyone but herself?

*Could Suzanne know about the magic wind?*

"Two years ago, I wished for a baby sister," Suzanne continued. "And I got one. You all know what a pain Heather is. Having a baby in the house is *nothing* like I thought it would be."

*Phew*. Katie smiled. What a relief. Suzanne didn't know about her secret after all.

Just then, Louie came over with their pizza. "Here you go, gang," he said as he put the tray on the table. "A Christmas special."

Katie looked down at the pie. Louie had arranged spinach leaves in the shape of a Christmas tree. He'd cut mushroom slices into small pieces and placed them like

ornaments on the spinach-leaf tree.

*Mmmm*, Katie thought. *This pizza looks great!*

"It's so Christmassy!" Suzanne exclaimed.

"I'm starving!" George declared as he started to grab a slice of pizza. "Louie, can we have some paper plates, please?" he asked.

Louie walked over to the counter and grabbed six dishes.

"What are these for?" George asked him.

"To put your pizza on," Louie replied.

"What happened to the *paper* plates?" Kevin asked.

"I'm not using them anymore," Louie replied. "I'm trying to save some trees."

"Huh?" George asked.

"Paper is made from trees," Louie explained. "The earth needs trees to keep the air and land healthy. I don't want any trees to have to die just so I can use paper plates. *These* plates can be washed and used again and again."

"They're kind of like your Christmas present to the planet," Katie told him.

Louie grinned. "Exactly."

"Merry Christmas, Earth," Katie said as she put a slice of pizza on her plate.

# Chapter 2

"More latkes, Katie?" Mrs. Fox asked as she held up a platter of fried potato pancakes.

"No thank you," Katie replied. She was really full. First she'd eaten three slices of Christmas pizza at Louie's for lunch. Now, here it was dinnertime, and she had just finished a whole stack of potato pancakes at Jeremy's house.

"Try them with the applesauce," Jeremy suggested. "Latkes and applesauce go great together."

"Okay, maybe just one more," Katie agreed. She took another pancake from the tray. "Do you eat these every night of Hanukkah?"

"Some people do," Mrs. Fox told Katie. "But we eat them only on the first night of Hanukkah."

"I'd never fit in my pants if we had these for eight nights in a row," Mr. Fox joked. He rubbed his chubby belly. "I wonder if this is how Santa Claus got his belly."

"I never heard of latkes at the North Pole," Katie answered. "I think Santa's stomach is full of cookies."

"Santa doesn't know what he's missing," Mr. Fox teased. He speared two more latkes from the platter.

Mrs. Fox laughed. "I'm so glad your mother agreed to let you spend the first night of Hanukkah with us, Katie," she said.

"Me too," Katie said. "I can't wait to see what gift Jeremy is getting tonight."

"Neither can I," Jeremy agreed excitedly. "I *really* can't wait!"

"Okay, I get the message," Mrs. Fox sighed. "But before we get the presents, why don't

we light the menorah? After all, it symbolizes what the holiday is about."

"Hanukkah is about the miracle of the oil," Jeremy told Katie.

Katie looked at him curiously. She didn't know what he was talking about.

"A long time ago, the Jews fought a big war against the Greeks," Jeremy explained. "They won the war, but their temple was left a mess. Even the holy lamp—the one that was supposed to always stay lit—wasn't burning anymore. The Jews had enough oil to light the lamp for just one day. But somehow, that oil burned for *eight* days. It was a miracle."

"That's exactly right, Jeremy," Mr. Fox said proudly.

Katie followed Jeremy over to the kitchen counter where Mrs. Fox had placed a silver candleholder. There were spots for nine candles. But Mrs. Fox had placed only two candles in the holder—one on the end and one in the middle.

"We use the candle in the middle to the light the others," Mr. Fox explained. "Tonight we are lighting the first candle, because it's the first night of Hanukkah. Tomorrow we'll light two candles. And then three. By the eighth night, the whole menorah will burn brightly."

Mrs. Fox lit the Hanukkah candle and said some prayers in Hebrew. Then she went into the hall closet and pulled out a huge box covered in silver-and-blue wrapping paper.

"This is from Grandma," she told Jeremy.

"Awesome!" Jeremy cheered. "My grandma always knows exactly what I want. She gets me the best gifts."

"Wow," Katie said. The box was big enough to hold a small snowboard. "Open it," she urged as she crossed her fingers for luck.

Jeremy smiled broadly as he tore off the wrapping paper and yanked the box open.

But his smile soon turned to a frown. "It's a coat," he said quietly.

"Not a *coat*," Mrs. Fox told him. "A ski

jacket. It's got lots of pockets, and it's very warm. But it isn't very heavy."

Jeremy fingered the shiny black material. "I guess Grandma doesn't always know what I want."

"Jeremy!" Mrs. Fox scolded.

"I mean, it's really nice," Jeremy corrected himself.

"You'll call her later and thank her?" Mrs. Fox reminded him.

"Sure," Jeremy answered.

Katie felt bad that her best friend was disappointed with his gift. "You're going to look so cool in that coat," she said, trying to make Jeremy feel better. "You should definitely wear it to school on Monday. You'll look like a professional snowboarder."

"A snowboarder without a snowboard," Jeremy groaned.

"You never know," Katie said. "You still have seven more nights of Hanukkah. Maybe you'll get a snowboard tomorrow."

That perked Jeremy up. "You really think so?" he asked her.

"Would you two like to play dreidel?" Mrs. Fox interrupted. She pulled out a little clay top with four sides. Each side had a Hebrew letter on it. "You get to eat whatever you win," she continued as she handed them each a bag of chocolate money.

"Yum!" Katie exclaimed. "Playing games with chocolate money. Now this is *my* kind of holiday!"

# Chapter 3

Usually, Sundays were lazy days in Katie's house. Her parents liked to sleep late, then read the newspaper and drink coffee. Katie played with Pepper, hung out with her friends, or read a book.

But this Sunday, the Carew house was bustling. Katie's dad was busy putting up Christmas lights. Katie and her mom were placing the finishing touches on their tree. Pepper was happy just sitting on the couch and sniffing the air. It smelled like a mix of pine and gingerbread.

"These gifts look really pretty," Katie said as she looked at the pile of presents beneath the tree. She pointed to a box that was wrapped in shimmery blue foil. A small, folded paper swan sat on top of the box. It looked like the swan was swimming on a beautiful icy pond.

"Lauren, the new gift wrapper at Thimbles Department Store, is amazing," Mrs. Carew said as she walked into the living room with a box of ornaments for the tree. "Everything she does looks like a piece of art."

Katie picked up another box. It was wrapped in green and red paper. In the center, Lauren had placed tissue paper folded into the shape of a poinsettia flower. "That one's almost too pretty to open," Mrs. Carew said.

*"Almost,"* Katie agreed. "But I'm still dying to know what's inside. Maybe I could open just this one."

Mrs. Carew chuckled. "There are just a few more days until Christmas, Katie."

"But Jeremy has already opened one of his gifts. And he'll get another one tonight. And another the next night, and . . ."

"That's because he celebrates Hanukkah," Mrs. Carew interrupted her. "We open our gifts on Christmas morning. That's how we have always done it."

She placed a small white dove ornament on a branch of the tree. "There. I think we're finished. Take a look."

"Wow!" Katie exclaimed.

The tree was so tall, it almost reached the ceiling of the living room. Red and green lights shimmered among its branches. And there were *so* many ornaments. Some were really old, like the snowman ornament that had been Katie's mom's when she was a little girl.

Other ornaments were brand-new, like the fuzzy cocker spaniel Katie's grandmother had made for her.

Some were very traditional, like the angel on the top of the tree.

And others were just plain silly—like the

Rudolph ornament Katie's dad had hung near the top of the tree. Its giant red nose blinked on and off.

"I have a few more gifts to put under the tree," Mrs. Carew told Katie.

"Any for me?" Katie asked her.

"Could be," Mrs. Carew answered mysteriously.

"Ruff! Ruff!" Pepper barked suddenly.

"Don't worry, Pepper," Katie told him. "I have a present for you, too. In fact, I'm going upstairs right now to wrap it."

Katie stood up and walked toward the stairs. Pepper followed close behind.

"You can't come with me," Katie told him. "Your gift is supposed to be a surprise."

But Pepper wouldn't listen. He kept following Katie up the stairs.

"Mom!" Katie cried out. "Could you keep Pepper down there with you? I want to wrap his present."

"Pepper, come here," Mrs. Carew called. "I

have a special treat for you."

At the sound of the word *treat,* Pepper raced toward the kitchen. That gave Katie just enough time to run upstairs and lock herself in her room.

Quickly, she pulled the new chew toy from her closet. Then she laid out a few sheets of Christmas wrapping paper and pulled tape and scissors from her desk drawer.

"This is going to be the most beautiful gift under the tree," she told herself as she began to cut the wrapping paper in the shape of a Christmas tree.

✕ ✕ ✕

An hour later, there were scraps of wrapping paper all over Katie's bedroom. Katie had tape all over her clothes and hair.

But the Christmas tree–shaped chew toy was still unwrapped.

Katie had discovered that it wasn't so easy wrapping Pepper's present. It was a really weird shape. Every time Katie tried to close one end of the paper, another part would tear or rip.

No matter what she did, Katie couldn't get Pepper's gift to look as nice as the gifts from Thimbles Department Store did.

"Grr," Katie grumbled loudly as she struggled to tape another piece of paper to the chew toy.

*Squeak!* The toy seemed to yell back at her as she pressed down on it to wrap.

"Will you be quiet?" Katie shouted at the toy.

"Are you okay in there?" Katie's mother called from the hallway.

Katie blushed. It was embarrassing to be caught talking to a doggie chew toy!

"Sure," she said quickly. "I'm just finishing up with Pepper's gift."

"Do you need help?" Mrs. Carew asked.

Katie probably could have used some grown-up help. But she was determined to wrap Pepper's present all by herself.

"No thanks, Mom," she told her. "I've almost got things wrapped up in here."

Katie put the last bit of tape on the top of the gift. She sat back and looked at her work. The chew toy was sealed up tightly, but it was also a mess. She hoped Pepper wouldn't mind.

A little while later, the phone rang. It was Jeremy.

"Did you get your snowboard?" Katie asked him excitedly.

"No, not tonight. But I'm pretty sure the snowboard will be next," Jeremy answered.

"Why?" Katie asked.

"Tonight, I got these awesome snow goggles from my cousins. I think my family is making sure I have all the right clothes so that when I get the snowboard, I'm ready to go."

"I hope you're right," Katie told him.

"I know I am. I'll be snowboarding over vacation," Jeremy said confidently.

"If it snows," Katie reminded him.

"Oh, it will," Jeremy assured her. "It *always* snows during winter vacation!"

*Vacation.* Katie adored that word. And the day after tomorrow it would be here!

# Chapter 4

Katie loved the way class 4A looked at Christmastime. Her teacher, Mr. Guthrie, had decorated the room to look like the North Pole. There was an igloo made of Styrofoam bricks near the blackboard. White paper snowflakes hung from the ceiling. Colorful Christmas lights framed the windows.

There was a Hanukkah menorah on the windowsill. Beside it sat another candleholder. But this one held seven candles. Katie had never seen one like that before.

No doubt about it. Everything you could want for the holidays was in that classroom. But as Katie sat down in a beanbag chair, she noticed that something very important was missing . . .

*Their teacher!*

"Where's Mr. G?" Katie asked her classmates.

"Do you think he's absent?" Emma Stavros asked.

"No way," Mandy Banks answered her. "Mr. G. is never absent."

Just then an old woman with a big pointy nose burst into the classroom. She was wearing a long robe and a scarf over her head.

"Hello, everyone," she greeted the kids in a deep voice.

"Hey, that's Mr. G!" Andy Epstein said, laughing.

"Why are you dressed like that?" Kadeem Carter asked their teacher.

"I'm not Mr. G. I'm La Befana!" the person in the robe and scarf answered.

But the kids weren't fooled. Not for a minute.

"Very funny, Mr. G.," George said, laughing. "Good one."

But Mr. G. wasn't admitting that the kids were right. "I'm La Befana," he insisted again. "And I'm getting ready to give all the good girls and boys in Italy presents . . . but not until January sixth."

Katie stared at Mr. G. Her teacher had done some weird things before. But this was definitely the weirdest!

"They don't get gifts in Italy until January sixth?" George asked.

"That's right," Mr. G. told him. "In Italy, the big gifts are delivered by La Befana, instead of Santa. And they don't come until January."

"That's weird," Kevin said.

"Your Christmas customs would seem weird to kids in Italy," Mr. G. told him. "Different countries have different traditions." He took off his fake nose, untied his head scarf, and slipped out of his robe.

"Why do I get the feeling we're about to have another learning adventure?" George said.

"Because we are!" Mr. G. announced excitedly. "We're going to go around the world, Christmas style!"

With that, the teacher pushed a button on his CD player. Strange bagpipe music began to play.

"That's traditional Italian Christmas music," he said. "It's played when La Befana comes to town with the gifts."

"I'll have to remember to give Louie a present on January sixth," Katie whispered to Emma Weber. "His family is from Italy, you know."

"In Italy, it's cold at Christmastime," Mr. G. continued. "But down in Australia, December is summertime. Families there celebrate Christmas with beach picnics and backyard barbecues." He reached behind the igloo and pulled out a beach ball. He hit the ball toward Kadeem.

Kadeem hit the ball to Emma W.

She hit the ball to Katie.

Katie hit the ball to George. She smiled happily. Christmas in Australia was fun!

Emma S. waved her hand high. "I know what they do for Christmas in Greece," she told Mr. G. "My grandma was born there."

"Tell us about it," Mr. G. said excitedly.

"They sing *kalandas*," Emma S. explained. "They're kind of like Greek Christmas carols. My brother and I sing them with our family. And we get our presents on January first, because that's when they exchange gifts in Greece."

"That's really interesting, Emma," Mr. G. said. "It's nice to keep family traditions."

"My family has a cool tradition, too," Kadeem said. "We celebrate Christmas *and* Kwanzaa."

"Did you see the *kinara* on the windowsill?" Mr. G. asked him. He walked over and picked up the candle holder that had seven holes.

"We have one at home that my dad made," Kadeem told the teacher. "We'll start lighting it on the day after Christmas, when Kwanzaa starts."

"What is Kwanzaa?" Mandy asked.

"It's a holiday that's based on celebrations they have in Africa," Mr. G. explained. "The name *Kwanzaa* comes from a Swahili word that means 'first fruits of the harvest.' "

"We light one candle a night for seven nights," Kadeem told his friends.

"Do you get a present every night?" George asked him.

Kadeem nodded.

"Wow! So you get Christmas presents *and* Kwanzaa presents?" Katie exclaimed. "You're lucky." She sounded a little jealous.

"The Kwanzaa presents are usually hand-made," Kadeem explained. "They're supposed to be educational. Kwanzaa's not really about the presents. It's supposed to be about connecting to your African roots."

"Christmas isn't supposed to be about presents, either," Emma W. said. "It's supposed to celebrate the birth of Jesus."

"We sometimes forget about the true meaning of the holiday season," Mr. G. said.

"Like peace on Earth," Emma W. said.

"And kindness," Mandy added.

"And family traditions," Andrew suggested.

"Exactly," Mr. G. agreed. "This time of year, those things are celebrated all over the world. Even here in Cherrydale. In fact, I think it's time we had a traditional Cherrydale holiday celebration right now! Everybody line up and get ready!"

The kids all stared at one another. What was Mr. G. up to now?

# Chapter 5

"Okay, everyone, sing out as loudly as you can!" Mr. G. ordered as he led the kids out into the hallway. "And stay together."

Katie couldn't believe it. Mr. G. had pulled them out of class . . . right in the middle of the school day. It wasn't even time for recess yet.

Even weirder, he was telling them to sing so loudly that they interrupted the other classes!

Well, not just sing, actually. Mr. G. was taking class 4A caroling.

"Mr. Kane isn't going to like this," Katie whispered to Emma W.

"Sure he will," Emma assured Katie. "Everyone likes carolers. Even school principals."

But Katie wasn't too sure. Mr. Kane liked rules . . . a lot. And one of his rules was no noise in the halls.

Still, Katie couldn't resist singing along with the rest of her class. She loved Christmas carols.

"On the second day of Christmas, my true love gave to me . . ." she sang loudly.

One by one, the teachers in the school opened their doors and welcomed the carolers. Most of them seemed happy to see the class.

The only teacher who seemed upset about the caroling was Mr. Starkey. That was *really* weird since Mr. Starkey was the school's music teacher.

"Wait a minute," Mr. Starkey shouted at class 4A. "Stop singing."

The kids quieted down and stared at him in surprise.

"You can't sing Christmas carols in the hallway," Mr. Starkey continued with a stern look on his face. Then he gave the fourth-graders a big smile. "At least not without these!"

Mr. Starkey reached behind him and picked up a huge box filled with bells. "Everyone knows you need to have jingle bells with you when you go caroling."

"Cool," Kevin said as he grabbed a pair.

"I just love the sound they make," Emma S. said as she took two wrist bells.

"Me too," Katie agreed. "They always remind me of Christmas."

"That's the point," Mr. Starkey said. He looked around to make sure all of the kids had bells. "Okay, now you're ready to go caroling. Have fun!"

"We will," Mr. G. assured him. "Let's go, gang! Jingle bells, jingle bells, jingle all the way . . ."

"Oh what fun it is to ride in a one-horse open sleigh," the kids in class 4A joined in as they walked through the halls.

Finally, the gleeful carolers reached the school's main office. Katie took a deep breath.

Any minute now, Mr. Kane would probably run out of his office to stop them.

Sure enough, a few seconds later Mr. Kane *did* come racing out into the hall. But he didn't get angry at all. In fact, he started laughing.

"Ho ho ho!" he chuckled.

Katie couldn't believe it. Mr. Kane, their school principal, was wearing a bright red Santa hat on his head. And he was laughing just like St. Nick.

"Ho ho ho!" he laughed again. "What have we here?"

"Carolers," Mr. G. answered. "We're starting a Cherrydale Elementary School tradition."

"How come you're wearing a Santa hat?" Kadeem asked the principal.

"Well, Santa's the big guy at the North Pole. And I'm the big guy at Cherrydale Elementary School," Mr. Kane explained. "We big guys should wear the same hat!"

That made sense to the kids.

"Are you here for a reason?" Mr. Kane asked them.

"We're here to sing," Mr. G. replied.

"Then let's hear it," Mr. Kane said.

That was all the encouragement the kids needed. They began shaking their bells and singing their songs.

"Rudolph the red-nosed reindeer had a very shiny nose," they sang out.

"And if you ever saw him, you would even say it glows," Mr. Kane joined in.

Katie could hardly believe it. The principal was standing in the middle of the hall, wearing a red Santa hat *and* singing!

The Christmas spirit sure was a powerful force!

# Chapter 6

The next morning, Katie woke up with a huge smile on her face. VACATION WAS HERE!

Katie dressed quickly and raced downstairs. She was ready to let the vacation fun begin. Today she was going to the mall for some last-minute Christmas shopping.

Mrs. Carew was going to be at the mall as well. But she wasn't nearly as happy about it as Katie was. That was because Mrs. Carew had to work all day. She was the manager of the Book Nook bookstore in the mall.

"This is the busiest time of the year at the store," she sighed as she put the coffee on the table. "All the last-minute shoppers will be coming in today. Not only will they be buying books, they'll be wanting them wrapped, too."

Mr. Carew nodded with understanding. "That takes a lot of work, dear," he agreed.

"Don't I know it," Mrs. Carew agreed. "And I'm not nearly as skilled at gift wrapping as Lauren at Thimbles is. You should see her. She makes it look so easy."

"It's a talent, all right," Katie's dad agreed.

✕    ✕    ✕

The mall was quiet when Katie and her mom arrived. It was still a few minutes before the shops opened. The store owners were the only ones there.

"Hey there, Katie," Louie said as he saw her walking toward the Book Nook. "Are you coming by for a special Christmas slice today?"

"Definitely!" Katie assured him.

"I've got Christmas plates," Louie told her. He held up a dish that had a picture of Santa on it. "I'm going to use these every year at Christmastime."

"I'll be back in time for lunch!" Katie promised him. Then she wandered off into the mall.

Katie walked around for a while. As the stores began to open, more and more people entered the mall. By the time Katie reached Thimbles Department Store—which was pretty far from the Book Nook and Louie's Pizza Shop—the mall was getting crowded.

Thimbles Department Store had a whole display of hats in the window. Katie knew she should go buy presents for her parents, but she couldn't help herself. Katie loved trying on hats.

She walked into the store and headed straight for the hat department. On the way, she passed the gift-wrapping counter. There was a long line of customers, all waiting for Lauren to work her magic on their presents.

Katie laughed when she saw Lauren. The

gift wrapper looked like a Christmas present! She was dressed in all green and red. There were little reindeer knitted into the back of her sweater. And on top of her head was a hair clip with a red bow on it.

Katie stopped for a minute to watch Lauren wrap a present. She was incredible. Her fingers flew across the green-and-red paper as she folded the edges down and neatly placed a piece of tape on each edge. Then she took a piece of shimmery silver paper and expertly folded it into a little star, which she glued to the center of the gift.

"That's gorgeous!" the woman who had bought the gift exclaimed.

Katie thought about the presents sitting under her tree at home. The ones from Thimbles looked beautiful because Lauren had wrapped them.

But Katie had wrapped Pepper's gift all by herself. *It* didn't look so beautiful. It was more like a lumpy blob of paper held together with

too much tape. And having it sitting there
next to all the beautifully wrapped gifts just
made it look worse.

Katie sighed. She wished she could unwrap
all the presents under her tree. That way
there wouldn't be any competition to see
which gift was wrapped the nicest.

And come to think of it, if there was no

gift wrapping, the Earth would get a pretty nice gift, too.

"What a waste," Katie said out loud.

"Excuse me?" a woman standing in the gift-wrap line asked her.

"I mean all that paper," Katie explained. "Why do we even bother wrapping presents? We just rip the paper off, anyway. And think of all the trees that had to die just so our presents can look good. Wrapping presents is ruining our environment. What kind of Christmas spirit is that?"

The woman looked at Katie curiously. She thought for a moment. "You know, you have a point," she said suddenly. "I can mail these without all that wrapping paper."

Katie smiled. "Exactly. And then you don't have to wait in this long line, either."

"Come on, Sally," the woman said to her friend. "This little girl is right. Wrapping paper is a waste."

"Save our trees," Katie said excitedly. She

smiled proudly as the women walked away. She felt like she had done something really wonderful.

But Lauren didn't feel that way. She had watched the women leave, too. And there was no smile on *her* face.

Katie felt kind of bad. She hadn't meant to upset Lauren. She'd just been trying to save the trees.

*Or was she?*

Deep down, Katie knew that wasn't exactly true. Actually, she had been kind of jealous of the way Lauren wrapped gifts. That was really why she had said what she did. The trees had just been an excuse.

Katie sighed. She sure had been feeling jealous a lot lately. And not just of Lauren. She'd also been pretty jealous of Jeremy and his eight Hanukkah gifts. And she'd been kind of jealous of the way Kadeem's family celebrated *two* holidays—Christmas and Kwanzaa.

Jealousy wasn't a very good feeling. In fact, she felt kind of miserable.

Katie turned and walked away. She didn't want to look at Lauren's sad face anymore.

# Chapter 7

As Katie walked through Thimbles Department Store, she was surrounded by last-minute shoppers. It was making her crazy. She didn't want to see any more gifts or any more people. She just wanted to be alone.

But that was hard to do on a crowded day in the mall.

In fact, there was only one place Katie could think of where she could be totally and completely alone . . . the dressing rooms at Thimbles!

Quickly, Katie grabbed a pretty pink-and-white striped sweater from a shelf and hurried toward the dressing room. Then she waited in the long line that led to the little closetlike dressing rooms.

It seemed to Katie that she was waiting an awfully long time for a dressing room to become free. But finally, she reached the front of the line.

Katie hurried into the little, private room. She locked the door and sat down on the bench.

*Phew.* It was nice to be alone for a second. Katie was tired of the mall being so crowded with holiday shoppers. She didn't like having to wait in line to buy things, get a snack, or just go to the bathroom.

She was sick of wrapping paper, presents, and her mom working late all the time.

In fact, Katie was just plain sick of Christmas! She couldn't wait for it to be over!

Just then, Katie felt a cool breeze blowing on the back of her neck. She gulped. There were no windows in the dressing room. So there was no way that draft was coming from outside.

Which meant only one thing.

The magic wind was back! And there was nothing she could do to stop it.

The magic wind began to circle wildly around Katie. Her red hair whipped around her head. The tornado swirled faster and faster. Katie shut her eyes tight and tried not to cry.

It seemed like the wind was blowing for a very long time. But it was probably just a few seconds. And then it stopped.

Katie knew what that meant. Switcheroo!

Katie wasn't Katie anymore. She was somebody else.

The question was, who was she?

× × ×

As soon as Katie opened her eyes, she saw a long line of tired-looking people standing in front of her. They were each holding something in their arms—a sweater, a blender, or a necklace. One man was even holding a vacuum cleaner!

"Lauren, could you fold a little origami Christmas tree for the middle of this package?" a woman asked as she handed Katie a baby doll in a box. "It's for my niece. And she's such a special little girl."

*Lauren?*

Katie turned around, hoping to see the talented gift wrapper standing behind her. But she wasn't there.

Oh, no! The magic wind had switcherooed Katie into Lauren. And all of these people wanted her to wrap their gifts . . . now!

Katie couldn't even wrap a toy for Pepper. What would she do with a vacuum cleaner? And she had *no* idea how to fold paper into the shape of a Christmas tree.

The customers in line were expecting to walk out of Thimbles with beautifully wrapped gifts. Katie was a *terrible* gift wrapper.

This was *so* not good!

# Chapter 8

"Lauren, could you hurry, please?" the woman with the doll urged Katie. "I still have to buy at least five more gifts today."

"Uh, well, I . . . I'm not sure . . ." Katie stammered.

"What's not to be sure of?" the woman asked. "Just do the same thing you did for me yesterday. You know, Christmas wrapping paper with a little paper tree on top."

Katie sighed. There was no way she could do that.

There was also no way she could get out of wrapping this woman's gift. That was Lauren's job. And Katie *was* Lauren. At least for now.

Katie was going to have to do her best. She walked over to the giant rollers and tore off a big sheet of red-and-green Christmas paper.

"I think that's a bit too much paper," the woman said. "It's not that big of a box."

"Hey, lady, let her do her job!" the man behind her in the line yelled. "She knows what she's doing."

"I was just . . ." the woman replied.

"The longer you stand there yapping, the longer we'll be waiting in this line," the man told her angrily.

"I beg your pardon?" the woman said, sounding just as angry as the man.

Katie gulped. These people certainly did not have the Christmas spirit. It sounded like they were about to start fighting. She had to wrap this gift quickly.

She laid the box down on top of the paper, just as she'd seen Lauren do. Then she tried to fold the corners up around the box.

But the woman had been right. There was

far too much paper. When she folded it over, the box looked lumpy.

Katie grabbed a pair of scissors and snipped off some of the wrapping paper. Then she tried to fold the remaining paper over the box.

But she'd cut off too much paper. Now there wasn't enough left to wrap the gift.

"I have to start over," Katie told the woman.

"Apparently," the woman said. She sounded really angry. Katie looked at the line. It seemed to be getting longer and longer by the second. And everyone seemed very impatient.

"What's the problem?" the woman with the doll asked Katie.

"You're making me n-nervous," Katie stuttered. "I . . . I can't think."

"Don't think. *Wrap!*" the angry man called out. "I gotta get home soon."

Katie walked over to the large rolls of paper and pulled hard on the red-and-green Christmas wrap.

*Whoosh! Bam!*

Katie had pulled too hard. The paper flew off the roller and knocked Katie to the floor. Now she was covered in a big roll of wrapping paper. She looked like a giant Christmas present.

"Oh, never mind!" the woman with the doll said. She grabbed her gift and stormed away from the gift-wrapping counter.

"I'm sorry," Katie apologized sadly. She struggled to unwrap herself.

"I'm glad *she's* gone," the man said. He hoisted the huge vacuum-cleaner box onto the counter. "Here. This is for my wife. Could you wrap it?"

Katie stared at the giant vacuum-cleaner box. "Um, well, I could try," she said.

"That pretty silver-and-gold paper would be nice," the guy continued. "My wife said she wanted something silver or gold for Christmas this year."

Katie had a feeling the man's wife had meant silver or gold jewelry, not a vacuum cleaner wrapped in silver-and-gold paper. But she went and pulled the silver-and-gold paper from one of the rollers, anyway.

Unfortunately, she couldn't figure out how to get the paper to stay where it belonged. No matter how much tape she used to hold the paper together, it kept tearing.

Katie worked for a really long time to make the gift look pretty. But in the end, it looked like a tall mountain of silver-and-gold wrapping-paper scraps held together with several rolls of tape.

Still, it was covered. Quickly, Katie grabbed a silver bow and slapped it on top.

"Here you go, sir," she said, handing the gift back to him.

"What a mess!" the man declared. "This doesn't look nice at all!"

He ripped off all the paper. Then he placed the bow back on the top of the gift. "There. That's better," he said as he walked away.

Katie sighed. She could have done *that*.

×　×　×

Things got worse the longer Katie worked at the gift-wrapping counter. She was making a mess of things. She'd used up almost all the paper on the rollers and had gone through mounds of tape. But none of the gifts she had wrapped looked pretty. People were very disappointed.

Katie had to admit that she would have been disappointed if she'd gotten one of those gifts, too. There was something wonderful about getting a present that was wrapped up all pretty and nice. It made Christmas morning extra special.

Katie finally understood. Christmas wrapping paper wasn't a waste after all. It was a really special part of the holiday.

*A part of the holiday she had ruined.*

# Chapter 9

Just then, a little man with a long nose and tiny glasses walked up behind Katie. He was wearing a badge on his jacket. It read, "Department Manager."

"What is going on here?" he demanded loudly.

Katie jumped. For a little man, he sure had a big mouth.

"Well, I . . ." Katie began.

"What a mess!" the manager interrupted. "And why are we all out of paper?"

"You see," Katie said, "there were all these weird gifts. Vacuum cleaners and baby dolls and . . ."

"This is just terrible," the department manager snapped. "It's the worst thing that could happen . . . ever!"

Katie could think of a lot worse things that could happen. But, of course, she didn't say that to the department manager.

"Lauren, go on your break now!" the manager told her angrily. "I'm going downstairs into the storeroom to get more paper."

Katie didn't need to be told twice. She turned and raced from the gift-wrapping counter.

As Katie hurried to get out of Thimbles, she saw lots of angry customers with badly wrapped gifts. They were all glaring at her.

Things weren't much better out in the mall. Lots of the people there recognized Lauren. And they all seemed to have heard about the mess she'd made at Thimbles.

Katie hated being stared at. She wanted to get away from all these people. But to do that, she would have to leave the mall and go outside.

Katie wasn't supposed to leave the mall without her mother. That was a *big* rule.

"There she is," Katie heard a woman in a blue hat say. She pointed right at Katie. "That woman made a total mess out of the gift I got my grandmother. She should be fired."

Tears started to stream down Katie's cheeks.

"Rules, schmules!" she shouted as she ran for the exit.

× × ×

Katie finally found a place where she could be totally and completely alone. It was a small alleyway behind the food court, near the Dumpsters. Nobody hung out there, ever. All that old, moldy, half-eaten food smelled too bad.

But Katie didn't care. The disgusting smell wasn't nearly as awful as the way people inside were treating her.

Katie plopped down on a huge pile of old newspapers wrapped up in a clear plastic bag. It wasn't fair. She had tried her best to make those presents look nice. It wasn't her fault that she didn't know how to wrap gifts. It wasn't her fault that she wasn't *really* Lauren.

It was all the magic wind's fault!

At that very moment, Katie felt a familiar breeze blowing on the back of her neck. She knew right away that it wasn't just an ordinary breeze.

The magic wind was back!

×

And it was getting stronger. Within seconds, it was whipping wildly around Katie. The tornado spun her around, faster and faster— like a crazy spinning top.

And then it stopped. Just like that.

The magic wind was gone.

And Katie was back!

# Chapter 10

Katie didn't wait around near the Dumpsters. Instead, she raced back into the mall.

It felt good not to be breaking her mother's rule anymore. It also felt good to be able to walk past the stores without anyone giving her a dirty look or yelling at her. After all, no one was mad at Katie Carew.

But plenty of people were still very angry at Lauren. The gift-wrapper was sitting all by herself in the food court, sipping a soda, and trying hard not to cry. But every now and then a tear would sneak out from the corner of her eye.

Katie began walking over to Lauren's table. She wanted to make her feel better. But before Katie could reach her, the department manager reached her table. And boy, did he look angry!

"There's no wrapping paper left in the storeroom!" he shouted at Lauren. "Which means Thimbles will not be wrapping any more gifts this holiday season! A lot of people are going to be disappointed. And it is all your fault!"

Katie gulped when she heard that last part. She knew it wasn't Lauren's fault at all.

"But, Mr. Snickering, I didn't . . ." Lauren began. Then she sighed. "Or maybe I did. I don't know what happened this morning."

"I do," Mr. Snickering told her. "You made a mess of our gift-wrapping counter. And since we have no more gift wrap, we have no need for you. *You are fired!*"

"But, Mr. Snickering," Lauren pleaded, "there must be *some* gift wrap left in the store that we can use."

Mr. Snickering shook his head. "There's no

paper anywhere."

"But I need this job," Lauren pleaded.

"Well, find some gift wrap, and you can have your job back," Mr. Snickering replied as he walked away. "Otherwise, don't come back to the store."

Katie stood there for a minute, unable to move. She felt awful for Lauren. She also felt really guilty. After all, it was Katie who had made the mess at the gift-wrapping counter.

So it was going to have to be Katie who made things right again! She took a deep breath and walked right up to Lauren.

"Hi," Katie said quietly.

Lauren looked sadly at Katie. "Oh, it's you," she said. "Well, you'll be happy to know that Thimbles won't be wrapping gifts anymore. They ran out of paper, and now I'm out of a job."

"That doesn't make me happy," Katie assured her.

"I thought you said I was destroying the

planet by wrapping gifts," Lauren reminded her.

"It isn't *your* wrapping that's ruining the Earth," Katie corrected her. "It's the wrapping *paper* that's doing it."

"How can you wrap gifts without *wrapping paper*?" Lauren asked her.

Katie thought about that for a minute. Then suddenly, she got a great idea.

"I know where you can find plenty of paper and still save trees!" she exclaimed suddenly. "Come with me! Let's get your job back!"

# Chapter 11

An hour later, Katie was back in the food court. But this time, she was carrying a big present. It was wrapped in old, thrown-out newspapers. But it didn't look like garbage. It looked fantastic.

Lauren had used the newspaper to make the package look like a palm tree. She'd attached tiny green and red bows to some of the newspaper leaves. They shimmered like Christmas lights on the tree.

The first people Katie bumped into in the food court were Jessica Haynes and her mom. "Did you see how they're wrapping gifts at Thimbles now?" Katie asked Jessica. "They're using recycled newspaper. This present is for my grandmother. It's a poster of a roller coaster."

"Why would they use old newspapers to wrap new presents?" Jessica asked.

Katie frowned. Jessica did not seem impressed. Neither did any of the other people sitting nearby. They all looked at Katie's package strangely and then turned away.

Katie really wanted people to like her idea for wrapping paper. She wanted them to go back to the gift-wrapping counter at Thimbles and have Lauren wrap their gifts, too.

Things were *not* going the way Katie had planned.

But Katie Carew was not the kind of kid who gave up. "Thimbles is giving a present to planet Earth," Katie told Jessica's mom. "Wrapping paper is made from trees. You have to cut down a lot of trees to wrap gifts."

Mrs. Haynes seemed interested. At least a

little bit. So Katie kept talking. She held up her newspaper–palm tree present. "This way, they're using paper twice," she said. "That means fewer trees have to be cut down."

Jessica didn't seem to care about the trees. But she did like the way Katie's gift looked. "Well, that is *kind* of neat," Jessica said as she looked at the present in Katie's hand. She ran her fingers over the palm tree's newspaper leaves. "How did Lauren do that?"

"I don't know," Katie told her. "But she's really talented. And you should see some of the other packages she's wrapped. One has these tiny paper birds all over it. They're made out of old comic strips. It's very colorful."

"I thought I heard Lauren had made a mess of things over at Thimbles," Mrs. Haynes mentioned.

Katie sighed. It hadn't been Lauren who had done that. It had been Katie. But, of course, she couldn't tell Mrs. Haynes about

her switcheroo. Mrs. Haynes never would have believed her anyway. Katie wouldn't have believed it, either, if it hadn't happened to her.

"Well, she's doing a great job now," Katie said.

Mrs. Haynes looked at the gift again. "It *is* interesting," she said slowly. "A package wrapped like this would stand out under the tree."

The woman at the next table looked over at Katie. "I couldn't help overhearing your conversation," she said.

Katie grinned. She was glad. In fact, she'd been talking extra loud so people *would* overhear.

"I think what Thimbles is doing is wonderful," the woman continued. She looked around at all the paper plates and cups at the food court. "There's too much waste in this mall. More stores should be recycling."

"You should eat your lunch at Louie's

instead of at the food court," Katie told her. "He's stopped using paper plates. He's saving trees, too. And his pizza is really yummy!"

"What a great idea!" the woman exclaimed. "You know, you should tell everyone about how Thimbles and Louie's are doing their part to help the planet."

Katie smiled. That was exactly what she planned on doing!

# Chapter 12

"What beautiful presents!" Mrs. Carew exclaimed as Katie placed two more gifts under the tree later that evening. Inside one of the beautifully wrapped boxes was a scarf for her mother. The other held a big coffee mug for her father.

"I wrapped them myself," Katie told her mom. "Lauren showed me how to make the little birds. They're called cranes."

"You know, lots of people had newspaper cranes on their presents today. You wouldn't believe how many people came by with packages from Thimbles," Mrs. Carew said. "They loved the way Lauren was wrapping gifts in recycled newspapers. I don't know how she came up with such a wonderful idea!"

Katie smiled. She knew where Lauren had gotten the idea. But she wasn't telling.

"Wow, the snow is really coming down," Katie's father said as he looked out the window. "It's going to be good sledding weather tomorrow!"

Just then, the phone rang. Katie leaped up to get it.

"Hello," Katie answered.

The person on the other end didn't say hello back. He just screamed excitedly.

"Guess what? I got it!" he shouted into the phone.

Katie laughed. It was Jeremy. And she didn't have to ask what "it" was. She knew it was his snowboard.

"Not so loud," Katie said, holding the phone away from her ear.

"Oh, sorry," Jeremy said. "I didn't mean to yell."

"It's okay; I have another ear," Katie joked.

"I'm just so excited!" Jeremy exclaimed. "I can't believe I have my very own snowboard."

"I think that's great," Katie told him. And she really meant it. She wasn't jealous of Jeremy at all. She was happy for him.

"And it's snowing outside right now!" Jeremy continued.

"I know. My dad said it's going to be great sledding weather tomorrow," Katie told him.

"Sledding or *snowboarding*," Jeremy added. "That's why I'm calling you. Tomorrow night is Christmas Eve. And your mom is working during the day."

"Only until three o'clock," Katie explained. "I'm going to the mall with her. I guess I'll hang out at Louie's or something until she's finished with work."

"But my mom said you can come over *here* tomorrow morning instead," Jeremy explained. "Then we can both try my new snowboard."

"Wow! I've never been on a snowboard

before," Katie said.

"Me, neither," Jeremy admitted. "We can learn together."

"Are you sure you want to share your new present with me?" Katie asked him.

"Sure," Jeremy said. "That's what the holidays are about."

Katie looked over at the gifts under her tree. She was pretty sure that the small box in the corner had a new computer game in it.

"I think I'll have some presents to share with you, too," she told him. "I'll find out on Christmas morning."

"Cool," Jeremy said. "So you'll come over here tomorrow?"

"Hold on," Katie said. Then she shouted into the living room. "Mom, can I go to Jeremy's tomorrow morning instead of the mall?"

"Sure," Mrs. Carew agreed. "As long as his mother doesn't mind."

"I can come!" Katie told Jeremy happily.

"Cool. See you tomorrow," Jeremy said.

After she hung up with Jeremy, Katie walked back into the living room. The tree was brightly lit. The room smelled like pine needles and Christmas cookies. And there was so much snow falling outside. Everything seemed so Christmassy.

Suddenly, Katie didn't care about the crowds in the mall and all the lines she'd had to wait in all day. That was part of Christmas. Just like wrapping gifts, baking cookies, spending time with friends, and singing Christmas songs.

"Deck the halls with boughs of holly," she began to sing.

"Fa la la la la, la la la la," her parents chimed in.

"AROOOOO!" Soon, even Pepper was singing.

Katie gave her dog a big hug. She smiled at her parents. There was a lot of love in her living room. That was the best Christmas present she could have . . .

And it didn't need any gift wrap at all!

# The Santa Switch

# Chapter 1

"Okay, Katie, it's your turn," Mr. Guthrie said. "Whose Secret Santa will you be?"

Katie looked at the red-and-white Santa Claus hat her teacher was holding. Inside were lots of folded pieces of paper. Each paper had a name written on it. The person whose name she picked would be the person she would have to buy gifts for. That was how Secret Santa worked.

"I hope you get my name," Emma Weber whispered as Katie stuck her hand into the hat. "You'd be a great Secret Santa."

Katie hoped she picked Emma's name from the hat, too. Emma was one of her closest

friends. It would be easy to buy presents for her.

Katie reached all the way down to the bottom of the hat and pulled out one of the slips of paper. Then she slowly opened it and read the name:

KADEEM CARTER

Oh, well. She was just going to have to think a little harder to come up with good gifts.

"Okay, now that everyone has picked a name, I'll tell you the rules," Mr. G. said. "You will have to buy the person whose name you drew three gifts. The first two gifts should cost no more than one dollar each. The third present is the big gift. You may spend up to five dollars on that one."

Katie did the math in her head. Seven dollars. That was three more than she had in her bank at home. It would be Sunday until she would get her allowance. She sure hoped Mr. G. would give them some time before the first Secret Santa day.

"We'll start our Secret Santa gift exchanges next Tuesday. That's one week from today," Mr. G. told the class.

*Phew.*

"When you come to school, drop your gift in the big red bag outside the classroom door," Mr. G. continued. "You should wrap your presents in plain brown paper. And make sure you write the name of the person you are giving the gift to on your package. The first two days, I'll hand the gifts out for you. That way you Santas can stay secret until Thursday, when you reveal your identity to the person whose name is on your slip of paper."

"This is going to be so cool!" George exclaimed.

"I can't wait to go shopping," Mandy Banks said. "I know exactly what to buy for my person."

"Me, too," Emma Stavros agreed. "This is easy."

Katie wished she had it easy. *Kadeem.* That was a tough one. It was hard knowing what to buy for a boy. And it was even harder because this was the first year she and Kadeem had been in the same class. She didn't know him nearly as well as some of the other kids.

"Okay, gang, let's get this day rockin'

and rollin'," Mr. G. said. Katie knew she would have to think about her Secret Santa gifts later. Now she had to concentrate on her school work. "We'll start with social studies," he told the class. "Who can tell me about some of the animals that actually live at the Arctic Circle?"

George Brennan raised his hand high. "Ooh. Ooh. Ooh!" he shouted. "Mr. G., I know this one," he said excitedly.

Katie looked over at George and smiled. He was practically bouncing out of his beanbag chair. George really liked geography a lot. He was so excited, he knocked his backpack over. All his books and papers spilled out onto the floor.

"Check it out. George is Santa Klutz!" Kadeem joked.

Everyone laughed. Everyone except George, that is.

"What does Santa like to put into his cookies?" George asked the class.

"What?" Kevin Camilleri wondered.

"His teeth!" George exclaimed. Then he laughed. "Ho ho ho!"

Almost everyone else in the class laughed, too. But not Kadeem.

"What do Santa's elves learn in first grade?" Kadeem asked.

"What?" Andrew Epstein called out.

"The elf-abet!" Kadeem shouted.

"Hey, good one, dude!" Andrew said.

"Did you hear the one about Santa and—" George began.

"Whoa, hold on to that joke, dude," Mr. G. interrupted. "We can have a holiday joke-off this afternoon. But right now, we've got to stick to social studies."

Katie grinned. A joke-off! Now that was something to look forward to.

It also gave her a great idea. She knew exactly what Secret Santa presents she was going to get for Kadeem!

# Chapter 2

"Mom, I'm going over to Cinnamon's Candy Shop," Katie called up to her mom.

It was the Monday before the Secret Santa gift exchange was going to start. Katie finally had all the money she needed for Kadeem's gifts. She was buying the first two smaller gifts today.

Mrs. Carew was standing on a ladder, putting books on a high shelf in the fiction section of the Book Nook bookstore. She was the manager of the store. It was her job to make sure all the books were on the right shelves.

"Okay," Mrs. Carew called down to Katie.

"Just be back by five-thirty. I've got to get home and finish trimming the Christmas tree. Grandma is coming tomorrow, and I want everything to be just perfect."

Katie smiled. She couldn't wait to see her grandma. She was the most wonderful grandmother in the whole world.

Katie's grandma was the only adult Katie knew who rode roller coasters. She even had her own website with pictures of roller coasters from all over the world that she had ridden.

Katie's grandmother did other cool things, too, like swimming with dolphins in Mexico and skiing in the Swiss Alps!

Of course, she also did normal grandmother things, like baking cookies and knitting sweaters for people in her family.

Katie definitely couldn't wait to see her!

✕   ✕   ✕

The Cherrydale Mall was one of Katie's favorite places. Since her mother worked in the mall, Katie spent a lot of time wandering in and out of the stores. Almost all of the shopkeepers knew her. And even though they were grown-ups, they were all friends of Katie's.

The mall hardly ever changed. Sure, once in a while a new store or restaurant opened. But for the most part, everything stayed the same.

Except at Christmastime. Then the whole center of the mall was turned into a giant Winter Wonderland. It was complete with snow, reindeer, elves, and a little North Pole Express train that kids could actually ride!

And in the center of it all sat Santa Claus.

Of course, this wasn't a real Winter Wonderland. It was actually a photography studio in the center of the mall. Kids went there to sit on Santa's lap and have their pictures taken.

Katie watched one little boy being dragged onto Santa's lap by an elf. The kid definitely was not happy about it.

"I don't wanna go!" he screamed loudly.

"Come on, Jeffrey," his mother coaxed. "Just one picture."

"No!" Jeffrey shouted. "No Santa."

Katie was so busy watching Jeffrey's temper tantrum, she didn't even notice her best friend Suzanne Lock coming up behind her.

"What a brat!" Suzanne exclaimed, looking at Jeffrey.

Katie turned around. "I think he's just scared," she replied. "What are you doing here?"

"My mom's taking Heather to have her picture taken with Santa," Suzanne told Katie. She pointed toward the line of children and parents waiting to see Santa.

Katie spotted Mrs. Lock in the middle of the line. She was carrying Suzanne's one-and-a-half-year-old sister, Heather.

Heather was wearing a red velvet dress.

She had a big green bow in her curly brown
hair. "She looks so cute!" Katie told Suzanne.

"My mother bought her that dress just
to have her picture taken with Santa Claus,"

Suzanne explained. "She said I could have a new dress, too, if I would have my picture taken."

Katie studied Suzanne's outfit. She was wearing a pair of dark blue jeans, brown suede boots, and a yellow sweater with glitter around the neck and sleeves.

"I guess you said no," Katie said with a laugh.

"Of course," Suzanne told her. "I'm not going to the Winter Wonderland. That's totally for babies."

"I don't know, Suzanne," Katie told her. "It could be kind of cool to sit on Santa's lap. For old time's sake, I mean."

"It would not be cool," Suzanne told her. "I mean, look at that guy. He doesn't even look like the real Santa. His belly isn't nearly fat enough."

Katie shook her head. There was no point arguing with Suzanne when she got like this. "Well, I've got to get going," Katie said finally.

"I'm shopping for some of my Secret Santa presents."

"Oh, yeah, I heard you guys in class 4A were doing that," Suzanne replied. "Whose name did you pick?"

"I can't tell you that," Katie told her. "It's supposed to be a secret."

"Come on. I'm not even in your class," Suzanne urged. "And I'm your best friend."

"True," Katie agreed. "But you can't keep a secret. So I'm not telling."

Suzanne frowned. "Fine," she said. "But if I find out who got your name, I'm not telling you."

"That's okay," Katie answered. "I want to be surprised."

# Chapter 3

On Tuesday morning, Katie was the first one in the school building. She wanted to drop off her present before anyone could see her. By the time the other kids began placing their gifts in the big red bag, Katie was already seated on her beanbag chair.

"Okay, gang, let's get rolling," Mr. Guthrie said as he walked over to the board. "It's time to start learning."

"Oh," the kids all seemed to groan at once. It was obvious they wanted to get their Secret Santa gifts right away!

"Here's your WFT," Mr. G. said as he wrote on the board. WFT meant "Word for Today."

Each day, Mr. G. wrote a new, really hard vocabulary word on the board for the kids to learn.

"Today's word is *impetuous*," Mr. G. continued. "Can anyone tell me what that means?"

He looked around the room. Nobody raised a hand.

"George, why don't you look up the WFT in the dictionary for us?" Mr. G. suggested.

George walked over to the big red dictionary and opened to the *I* words. "Impetuous," he read out loud. "Acting on the spur of the moment."

"Now, someone use it in a sentence," Mr. G. said.

Andrew raised his hand. "I wish Mr. G. would be *impetuous* and let us do Secret Santa now."

Mr. G. chuckled. "That's right."

"No, I mean it," Andrew continued. "I really want you to!"

"Me too," Mandy added. "I'm dying to know what I got."

"Please, Mr. G.," Kevin pleaded.

Mr. G. rolled his eyes. But Katie could tell he wasn't really annoyed. He still had a big smile on his face.

"Okay, I surrender," he said finally. "We'll do Secret Santa now. But don't think you're off the hook. After you open your presents, it's back to work."

One by one, Mr. G. began handing out the gifts. "Don't be *impetuous*," he told them. "Please wait until everyone has a present before you open yours."

The kids waited until all the gifts were handed out. "Go for it!" Mr. G. shouted.

"Oh, cool!" Mandy squealed as she held up a small pin with two bells hanging from it. She pinned it to her shirt right away.

"I love this!" Emma W. said as she unwrapped a package of Bayside Boys trading cards. She smiled at Katie. "Only a good friend would know the perfect present to buy for me."

Katie shrugged, but didn't say anything. Obviously someone else knew Emma W. pretty well, too.

"What did you get?" Emma W. asked Katie.

Katie opened her present and found a round piece of red rubber. "What is this?" she asked.

"Whoa, check it out!" George cried out from across the room. "Katie Kazoo got a whoopee cushion!"

Everyone laughed.

Katie looked at the whoopee cushion and sighed. She wasn't the kind of kid to put that on someone's seat. The noise that came out of that thing would only embarrass the person who sat on it. Katie didn't like embarrassing people.

Obviously her Secret Santa wasn't someone who knew her very well. It was probably one of the boys—maybe George or

Kevin or Kadeem. They liked practical jokes.

"Sweet!" Kevin exclaimed, holding up a packet of tomato seeds. "I can grow my own tomatoes! Awesome!"

"Check out my gift," Kadeem called to everyone. "It comes with a joke." He looked at the riddle on top of his gift. "What kind of beans don't grow in a garden?" he asked everyone.

"What kind?" Andrew asked.

"Jelly beans!" he shouted out as he held up his present for everyone to see. He opened the bag and popped a bright blue one into his mouth. "Yum, blue raspberry!"

Katie smiled. Kadeem had really liked his gift. Boys weren't so hard to buy presents for after all.

# Chapter 4

"So what did your Secret Santa get for you?" Suzanne asked as she, Katie, and Emma W. walked home from school together later than afternoon. They were going to play at Katie's house.

Katie frowned. "A whoopee cushion. How dumb is that?"

"I think it's kind of neat," Emma W. said. "You could really do some funny things with that."

"Oh, yeah," Suzanne agreed. "You know what you should do? You should invite Mrs. Derkman over to your house, and then make sure she sits on it."

The girls all laughed at that. Mrs. Derkman was the strictest teacher in the entire school. Katie and Suzanne had suffered through an entire year with her when she was their third-grade teacher last year. Mrs. Derkman was also Katie's next-door neighbor. Katie just couldn't get rid of her.

"That would be funny," Katie agreed. "Imagine Mrs. Derkman letting out a noise like that!"

The girls giggled again.

"Hey, check out those motorcycles," Suzanne said. She pointed toward Katie's house.

"Yeah!" Katie exclaimed. "My Grandma is here!"

"Your grandmother rides a motorcycle?" Emma W. asked, amazed.

"Uh-huh." Katie nodded proudly. "That red one is hers. Isn't it beautiful?" Her grandmother had e-mailed her a picture of the motorcycle. But it was even cooler-looking in real-life!

"Do you think she'd take you for a ride on it?" Emma asked.

Katie shook her head. "My mother says I have to wait until I'm older. A lot older. She doesn't really like motorcycles."

"Katie's mom isn't nearly as cool as her grandmother is," Suzanne told Emma. "I've known Katie's family a long time."

Katie sighed. Suzanne loved to remind Emma that she had been Katie's friend much longer than Emma had.

"Who does the other motorcycle belong to?" Emma wondered.

"I don't know," Katie admitted. "Grandma must have brought a friend. Come on, let's go inside."

The girls all raced up to the front porch.

"Grandma!" Katie shouted as she entered the house.

A small woman with bright red hair and

freckles just like Katie's came running to greet her. Katie leaped into her grandmother's arms.

"It is so great to see you, Kit Kat," Katie's grandmother said.

"Wow, you guys really look alike," Emma blurted out. "Your hair's the same color and everything."

"Except my color comes out of a hair-dye bottle," Katie's grandma admitted. She smiled at Katie's friends. "Suzanne, it's so good to see you again. You've gotten so tall. Just like a model."

Suzanne struck a pose. She tilted her head and smiled brightly as though there were a camera in the room. "I have been doing some modeling," she said.

"You've been taking modeling *classes*," Katie corrected her.

"Same thing," Suzanne insisted.

It really wasn't the same thing. But Katie didn't feel like wasting her time talking about that now. She wanted to spend time talking to her grandmother.

"This is Emma Weber," Katie said. "We're in the same class at school."

"Nice to meet you, Emma," Katie's grandmother said. "Come on in. I have a friend here, too. I want to introduce you."

The girls followed Katie's grandma into the living room. Katie saw her mom sitting on the couch near the Christmas tree. And next to her was a white-haired man with a chubby belly and a long white beard. He was wearing small round glasses, a thick black motorcycle jacket, jeans, and big black boots.

"Girls, this is my friend Nick," Katie's grandmother said.

Nick stood up and walked over to Katie. "You have to be Katie. You look just like your grandmother!"

"You're right," Katie told him. "And these are my friends Suzanne and Emma."

"Hi, girls," Nick said.

Suzanne and Emma didn't answer. They just stood there, staring at Nick.

Katie looked at them strangely. She couldn't believe they were being so rude.

"Um, are there any Christmas cookies?" Katie asked, trying to break the silence in the room.

"Of course," Katie's mom said. "Grandma brought them."

"Great!" Katie said. "Did you make any of the Rudolph-shaped ones? You know, the ones with the little red candies on their noses?"

"Of course, Kit Kat," Katie's grandmother assured her. "I know how you love your reindeer cookies."

"Your grandmother and I met some reindeer," Nick told Katie. "Last summer, when we were on vacation in Finland."

"Real reindeer?" Katie asked, amazed.

"Yep," Nick told her. "They actually have reindeer farms there."

"The reindeer are so adorable," Katie's

grandmother added. "And gentle. They walked right up to Nick and ate out of his hand."

Nick threw back his head and laughed loudly. "Reindeer love sugar cubes," he told them.

"The reindeer probably recognized him," Suzanne blurted out.

Katie looked at her curiously. "Huh?" she asked.

"Um, nothing," Suzanne mumbled. "Can we go get those cookies?"

"They're in the kitchen," Mrs. Carew told Suzanne.

Suzanne grabbed Katie's and Emma's hands and pulled them out of the room as fast as she could.

# Chapter 5

"What's the matter with you guys?" Katie asked as soon as the girls were in the kitchen.

"What's the matter with *us*?" Suzanne replied. "How about *you*? You acted like you didn't even notice."

"Notice what?" Katie asked.

"You know," Emma said. "Nick."

"What about Nick?" Katie asked.

"Didn't you think there was something kind of . . . well . . . weird about Nick?" Emma suggested.

"Come on, guys. What's going on?" Katie was starting to lose her patience.

"He doesn't remind you of anyone?"

Emma continued.

Katie thought for a moment. "No," she said finally.

"Think about it, Katie," Suzanne said. "He's got that big belly and the white beard . . ."

"And how about those glasses?" Emma continued.

"And his laugh," Suzanne said. She threw back her head, stuck out her stomach, and laughed the way Nick did. "Ho ho ho!"

Katie stared at her friends. Now she got it. "You mean you guys think Nick looks like Santa Claus?"

"Don't you?" Suzanne asked. "Come on. You have to admit it was a little weird that the reindeer would just walk up to him and make friends."

"You heard him," Katie insisted. "It was because of the sugar cubes."

"That's what he *says*," Suzanne replied. "But you never know. Maybe he doesn't want anyone to know his true identity."

Katie shook her head. "Give me a break. He's just a friend of my grandmother's. I mean, think about it. Santa rides a sleigh. Nick got here on his motorcycle. And when was the last time you saw Santa Claus wearing a black leather motorcycle jacket?"

"I'm just saying it's possible," Suzanne said with a shrug.

"No, it's not," Katie told her. "You're being ridiculous."

Emma nodded. "Katie's right," she told Suzanne. "Nick's just a nice old guy who is visiting her for Christmas."

"Maybe," Suzanne answered. "But you've got to admit, it would be really cool if Santa Claus was actually sitting out there in the living room."

# Chapter 6

When Katie got to school on Wednesday morning, a crowd of fourth-graders were already gathered in the yard. Katie could see Suzanne in the middle of the crowd. She was talking very quickly.

"What's up?" Katie asked as she walked toward the group.

"Suzanne's telling us all about how Santa Claus is staying at your house," Jessica Haynes explained.

Katie rolled her eyes. "Santa is not at my house," she assured Jessica.

"Katie's right," Kadeem said. "I mean, Santa Claus? Who still believes in that?"

"Well, you would if you saw this guy," Suzanne said. "The guy makes friends with reindeer!"

"So? I have animal friends, too! What about Pepper?" Katie insisted.

"Pepper is your dog, Katie," Suzanne reminded her.

"And he's my friend," Katie said. "What does that make me? The Easter Bunny?"

George started to laugh. "Good one, Katie Kazoo!"

"I'm coming to *your* house on Christmas Eve, Katie," Kevin said. "I'll bet you'll get your presents before anyone. You'll be Santa's first stop!"

Katie shook her head. "Forget about it," she said. "Nick is not Santa. Besides, he won't even be at my house on Christmas Eve. He's got some friends to visit that night."

"Of course he won't be there, Katie," Suzanne told her. "He's got to leave and deliver presents all over the world."

"Suzanne, cut it out!" Katie insisted
angrily. She was getting really upset. She
knew Suzanne didn't really believe Nick was
Santa Claus. She was just saying all this to
get attention.

Just then the school doors opened. It was time to go inside.

Katie was never so happy to get into her classroom.

× × ×

"Okay, gang, let's see what your Secret Santas have brought this time," Mr. G. said later that morning. He picked up his big red bag and began distributing gifts.

As soon as everyone was holding a present, Mr. G. said, "Okay, open them up!"

Emma W. was one of the first ones to open her gift. "Oh, cool!" she exclaimed. She slipped a small ring with a black stone on top of it onto her finger. The black stone turned yellow, then green, then bright blue.

"Ooh! It's a mood ring!" she exclaimed. She looked down at the small card that came with the ring. It showed what all the colors meant. "See, the color changed to blue because I'm in such a good mood."

Katie looked at her gift. She hoped it

would be as cool as Emma W.'s. She opened it up and pulled out . . .

A big blob of plastic throw-up.

"Yuck!" Katie shouted.

Kevin looked over. "Cool!" he exclaimed. "That's totally gross."

"You can really creep people out with that," George agreed. "You should put it on Suzanne's tray at lunch."

"Can you imagine her face if she saw that near her food?" Kadeem added, laughing.

Katie shook her head. She was pretty angry with Suzanne. But she wasn't angry enough to do that!

"Kadeem, open yours," Andrew urged.

Katie looked up from her plastic throw-up and watched as Kadeem opened his gift.

"Awesome. It's another joke!" Kadeem said as he looked at the piece of paper that was wrapped around the gift. "It says, 'Who is Dracula's favorite baseball player?' "

"Who?" Andrew asked.

"The bat boy!" Kadeem laughed. He ripped the paper off the gift. "Check it out!" he exclaimed. "Baseball cards!"

Katie was glad Kadeem liked his gift. The other kids seemed pretty happy with theirs, too.

George loved the glow-in-the-dark stickers he got.

Emma S. couldn't wait to use her new silly straw at lunch.

Andrew was excited to try out the new mini-magic trick his Secret Santa had bought for him.

Mandy was having a lot of fun playing with the kaleidoscope that had been in her package.

Katie looked from her make-believe vomit to the ring on Emma's finger. Emma's ring was bright blue. She was obviously happy with her present.

But Katie wasn't happy with hers. In fact, if she had been wearing Emma's ring, the stone would definitely be a cold, angry black!

# Chapter 7

"Plastic throw-up! Can you believe it?"
Katie shouted as she and Suzanne walked
through the mall on Wednesday evening. The
girls had met there after Katie's cooking class
and Suzanne's modeling class. They both
needed to buy holiday gifts.

"I told you that boys could be real jerks,"
Suzanne reminded her. "You're the one who
always says I'm wrong."

"Well, not all boys are jerks," Katie insisted.

"A girl would never have gotten you a
present like that," Suzanne said. "She would
have gotten you something pretty. Something
like that." Suzanne pointed to a hair clip that

was decorated with purple feathers. "That's what I'm going to buy for our class grab bag."

"But what if a boy picks it out of the bag?" Katie asked her.

"I don't care," Suzanne said. "I'm not going to buy a boy gift. No way!"

But Katie had to buy a gift for a boy. After all, she was Kadeem's Secret Santa. Luckily, she already had a plan.

"I'm getting my gift at my mom's store," she told Suzanne. "Why don't you do that, too? There are lots of books that both boys *and* girls would like."

Suzanne thought about that for a minute. "I could look, I guess."

"Cool," Katie said. She started walking toward the Book Nook. Suzanne followed close behind.

"Wow! Look at that line of kids waiting to meet Santa," Suzanne said as they walked past the Winter Wonderland. "Some of them sure don't look happy about it."

Katie shrugged. "I think they're unhappy about waiting in line for so long. Not about meeting Santa. Kids love Santa."

*Toot toot!* The North Pole Express train let out a loud whistle as it moved along the track in front of Katie and Suzanne.

"I wonder what's inside those boxes," Katie said. She pointed to the brightly wrapped gift boxes that sat in the train's caboose.

"I'll bet they're fake presents," Suzanne said. "Just like that Santa is fake. After all, everyone knows the real Santa is staying at your house."

That made Katie really angry. She was tired of Suzanne saying that Nick was Santa Claus.

"Nick is *not* Santa Claus!" Katie shouted.

"So, who is?" Suzanne asked her.

At that moment, the woman in the elf costume walked past them, holding a little boy's hand. Katie thought the elf looked like she was having a lot of fun. A lot more fun than

Katie was having arguing with Suzanne.

Katie looked closely at the elf. Her name tag read, "Ella the Elf." And the little boy whose hand she was holding looked really excited to meet Santa.

"Well, Katie?" Suzanne asked. "Who do you think Nick really is? Do you think that guy in the chair is the real Santa?"

"Don't you think I know that's just some guy in a Santa Claus costume?" Katie said. "But Nick isn't Santa either. The real Santa isn't here in Cherrydale!"

The little boy turned and stared at Katie. His face turned bright red. A tear fell down his cheek.

"THAT'S NOT SANTA!" he shouted at the top of his lungs. Then he turned and raced back to his mother.

Ella the Elf glared at Katie and Suzanne. "That wasn't nice," she scolded them. "Why do you big kids have to ruin this for the little ones?"

Katie felt terrible. "I'm really sorry," she apologized. "I didn't mean to ruin anything."

"Why don't you two get lost before you make some other kid cry," Ella told them.

"Come on, Katie," Suzanne urged. She pulled Katie by the arm. "Let's get out of here!"

# Chapter 8

"Thank you, Mrs. Carew," Suzanne said as she took the Book Nook bag in her hands. It had taken both Katie and Mrs. Carew to convince Suzanne to buy a book for her grab bag instead of the hair clip. But now Suzanne seemed pretty happy about it.

"You're welcome," Katie's mom said. "I think a kids' cookbook is a great grab-bag gift."

"I just love making people happy at Christmastime," Suzanne said.

Katie frowned. She and Suzanne sure hadn't made that little boy at the Winter Wonderland happy.

Suzanne had obviously forgotten all about that. But Katie hadn't. She still felt awful.

"Nobody's going to get that book unless I take you home so you can wrap it for the grab bag," Mrs. Lock reminded her daughter. She had met the girls at the bookstore a few minutes before.

"I know," Suzanne agreed. "You want a ride home, Katie?"

Katie would have liked to have gone home and spent extra time with her grandma. But there was still something she had to do.

"No thanks," she told Suzanne. "I have to get my last Secret Santa present."

✕ ✕ ✕

As soon as Suzanne was gone, Katie walked toward the back of the store. But before she could reach the section of the bookstore she was looking for, she heard a familiar voice.

"Mom, how much longer do we need to be here?" a boy asked.

Katie gulped. It was Kadeem! He was in the store!

"Hi, Katie," Kadeem greeted her. "What are you doing here?"

"Um . . . well . . ." Katie stammered nervously. "I'm . . . um . . . helping my mom," she lied.

"Cool," Kadeem said. "What do you do around here?"

Katie turned red. This was getting uncomfortable. She hated lying. "I, uh, do things in the stockroom," she said quickly. "In fact, I've got to go there right now. Bye!"

Quickly she ran off to hide in the stockroom of the store.

As she closed the door behind her, Katie breathed a sigh of relief. Kadeem wasn't allowed in the stockroom. Only people who worked at the store—and Katie—could go in.

"That was close," Katie whispered to herself. She sat down on top of a step stool and took a deep breath. It was nice to be alone for a minute.

Suddenly, Katie felt a cool breeze blowing on the back of her neck. Before she even had time to turn around, the breeze became stronger and stronger. Soon it was blowing like a wild tornado all around her.

Katie had wanted to relax. But obviously, the magic wind had other plans for her.

The magic wind became more powerful, whipping around Katie so quickly, she could hear it whistling in her ears. Her red hair blew all around, hitting her so hard in the face that she had to close her eyes.

And then it stopped. Just like that.

The magic wind was gone.

And so was Katie Carew. She had become somebody else. Switcheroo!

But who?

# Chapter 9

Katie knew without even opening her eyes that she wasn't in the Book Nook stockroom anymore. It was quiet in the stockroom. But it was really noisy here. People were talking, kids were screaming, and "Jingle Bells" was playing from a loudspeaker.

Slowly, Katie opened her eyes. She looked around. There was snow at her feet. But Katie wasn't cold at all. That was strange.

Katie bent down to feel the snow. Oh, that explained it. The snow wasn't real. It was just cotton.

Just like the snow in the Winter Wonderland at the mall.

As she bent down, Katie noticed her feet. She wasn't wearing her red high-top sneakers anymore. Instead, her feet were in green felt shoes that curled up at the top.

Elf shoes!

That could mean only one thing. Katie had become Ella, the elf at Winter Wonderland!

Suddenly, Katie felt a tug on the bottom of her short green skirt. She looked down to

see a little girl wearing a pink dress.

"Is it my turn to talk to Santa?" the girl asked in a squeaky voice.

Katie smiled. She was so cute! "It sure is," she said as she reached out for her hand.

The little girl seemed really happy. Katie was glad. It kind of made up for making that little boy cry earlier.

"Thank you," the little girl said as they reached Santa's chair.

"You're welcome," Katie replied. She stood beside Santa.

The little girl glared at Katie. "Could you leave us alone?" she asked. "This conversation is just between me and the big guy here."

Katie understood. She stepped back and began to head toward the line of children. As she walked away, she could hear the little girl say, "The first thing I want for Christmas is a new baby brother."

Katie smiled. How sweet was that?

"Because the baby brother you brought me

last year is a real pain," the little girl continued. "All he does is cry, sleep, and go to the bathroom. And he smells awful! This is not the baby brother I wanted at all. This year I want a brand-new model."

Katie sighed. Okay, so maybe the kid wasn't so sweet after all.

But there were plenty of other kids waiting to meet Santa. And plenty of others were going round and round in the North Pole Express.

Katie was sure most of the kids were as excited about meeting Santa as she had been when she was little.

At least she hoped so. Otherwise, this was going to be one super-terrible switcheroo!

# Chapter 10

"Which child would you like me to take up to Santa first?" Katie asked the mother who was standing at the front of the line. There were two boys standing next to her. They looked exactly alike.

"Me!" one of the boys shouted.

"Uh-uh. You always get to go first!" his brother shouted back.

"That's because I'm older," the first boy insisted.

"By five minutes," the other boy argued. "That doesn't count."

Their mother sighed. "Why don't you just take them together?" she told Katie. "That way, they won't fight about it."

"Okay," Katie said. She took the boys by their hands. "It's time to meet Santa," she told them.

"I get to ask for the red bike," one boy said.

"No way. You said you wanted a blue bike," his brother replied. "That means I get the red one."

"Does not!"

"Does too!"

Katie was very glad when she and the boys reached Santa's chair. Now they were his problem.

Santa didn't seem so happy about it, either. He just frowned and rolled his eyes as the boys argued over who would sit on Santa's right leg, and who would be stuck on his left.

*Oh, goodie, a baby!* Katie thought happily to herself as she spotted the next family in the line. After hearing the twins arguing, taking care of a kid who couldn't talk yet seemed great!

"It's Alison's first Christmas," the baby's proud father said. "We can't wait to get her picture taken with Santa Claus."

"She just drank a whole bottle," the baby's mother continued. "So she's not hungry. It will be easier for the photographer to get her to smile now."

"Good thinking," Katie told the parents as she took Alison from her father's arms and walked toward Santa Claus. "I'm sure her picture will look great!"

Alison was a pretty baby. But as Katie carried her down the snowy path to Santa's chair, she noticed something strange. While Alison's dad was holding her, her cheeks had been a pretty pink. But now her face was turning kind of green.

"Burp!" Alison let out a big, loud belch.

Suddenly, Katie felt something warm dripping down her neck and onto her shoulder. It smelled gross. Like spoiled milk.

Oh, no! Alison had spit up on her. Now

Katie had baby throw-up all over her neck. Yuck!

"Here," Katie said, handing Alison to the Winter Wonderland Santa.

"Hey, this kid's got a full diaper," Santa groaned. "I told you elves, I don't want them on my lap if they have a dirty diaper."

Katie was shocked. That wasn't Santa-like at all. Suzanne had been right! This guy was a really lousy fake Santa Claus.

"Here! Take her," the Santa Claus said. As he held out the baby, he turned his head away.

Katie had no choice. She took Alison in her arms and carried her back to her parents. It was pretty gross. The baby smelled like spoiled milk and dirty diapers, mixed together.

And to top it off, Alison had started to cry.

"What did you do to her?" Alison's mother demanded as she took her baby in her arms.

"Nothing," Katie said. "That Santa asked

me to bring her back to you because her diaper was dirty."

"*You* made her cry," Alison's father yelled at Katie.

"No I didn't," Katie assured him. "She's just crying because her diaper is full."

"This is awful," Alison's mother moaned. "Her first experience with Santa Claus, and you ruined it!"

"No," Katie insisted. She wrinkled her nose. Alison was really starting to stink. Katie took a big step backward. "I just . . ."

Toot Toot!

Just then, the North Pole Express came chugging by.

*Whoosh!* The model train swept Katie right off her feet. She had been so busy getting away from smelly baby Alison, she hadn't noticed that she'd stepped onto the train tack!

*Chugga chugga. Chugga chugga. Choo! Choo!*

The train kept circling around the track, carrying Katie along with it.

"Get this elf off of me!" a girl in the front seat shouted as Katie fell into her train car.

"Stop this thing!" Katie shouted even louder.

Boom! As the little engine went around a bend, Katie fell off the train. She banged her head on a plastic Christmas tree near Santa's chair.

*Clink. Clank. Clunk.* Three big star-shaped ornaments fell from the tree . . . and landed right on the fake Santa Claus's head.

"That's it!" he shouted. He leaped up from his chair and yanked his phony white beard from his face. "I quit!"

When the children saw the make-believe Santa take off his beard, they started to cry.

The grown-ups all began screaming at once.

Katie frowned. This was *so* not good!

# Chapter 11

The crowd of parents and children grew more and more upset. So did the photographer.

"Ella, what happened?" he demanded.

"Well, that baby really stunk, so I moved away, and I stepped onto the train track, and then the North Pole Express scooped me up, then I hit the tree and . . ." Katie began.

"No, not that," the photographer said angrily. "I saw that. I mean what happened to John?"

"John?" Katie asked. "Who's John?"

"The guy who was playing Santa," the photographer reminded her. He sounded kind of angry.

"Oh, him. He quit," Katie explained.

"This is awful," the photographer moaned. "I can't have a Winter Wonderland without a Santa Claus."

"Can't you hire somebody else to pretend to be Santa?" Katie asked.

"At this time of year?" the photographer asked. "All the really good Santa imperson-ators already have jobs."

"Well, maybe you can get John to come back," Katie suggested.

"I sure hope so," the photographer agreed. "But I can't leave now. I have to deal with all these angry people. You'll have to find him and talk him in to coming back to work."

"Me?" Katie asked. "Why me?"

"Because you gave him the dirty baby and hit him in the head with the ornaments," the photographer insisted. "Don't just stand here talking. Go! He shouldn't be too hard to find. Just look for the guy in the red velvet suit with a pillow stuffed in the belly."

As Katie walked away, she wondered what she could possibly say that would make John go back to playing Santa Claus. She just had to bring him back. The photographer, Ella, and all those children were depending on her.

What would the Winter Wonderland be without its Santa Claus?

Katie wandered through the mall, searching for John. But she didn't see him anwhere. It was like he'd magically disappeared or something.

She turned down a small hallway. It didn't have any stores in it, just a big door that led to one of the loading docks. She looked around to see if John was there. But the hallway was completely empty.

Katie stood there for a minute and leaned against the wall. A tear ran down her cheek. She felt really bad about ruining the Winter Wonderland for everyone.

Just then, Katie felt a cold, wintry breeze

blowing on the back of her neck. She turned quickly to see if the door that led to the loading dock was open.

Nope. It was shut tight. But there was definitely a wind blowing in the hallway.

That could mean only one thing. The magic wind was back!

Instantly, the magic wind picked up speed. It was blowing wildly now, circling faster and faster around Katie.

It was a cold wind. Like the kind you would find at the North Pole.

And then, suddenly, the magic wind stopped blowing. It had disappeared just as suddenly as it had come.

The wind was gone. But Katie was back!

She smiled. It was good to be wearing her own clothes again. She was happy not to smell like baby throw-up anymore.

Unfortunately, the photographer probably wasn't too happy right now. He still didn't have his Santa.

*At least not yet.*

Katie might not have found John, but she did know a way the photographer could have a Santa for his Winter Wonderland. She couldn't wait to tell him. Quickly she ran out of the hallway toward the center of the mall.

✕ ✕ ✕

By the time Katie had arrived back at the Winter Wonderland, most of the parents and children were gone. But the photographer was still there. And so was the real Ella.

"What do you mean you don't know what I'm talking about?" Katie heard the photographer demand. "I told you to go find John and talk him into coming back here."

"I—I sort of remember you saying some-thing about that," Ella said.

"Sort of?" the photographer shouted. "What do you mean, sort of?"

"The thing is, I don't really know what I remember," Ella explained. "It's all sort of fuzzy."

"Um . . . excuse me," Katie interrupted.

"Oh, no. It's you again," Ella said. "Didn't you and your friend cause enough trouble by telling that boy that the man in the chair wasn't the real Santa?"

Katie blushed. She still felt bad about that. "I didn't mean to talk so loudly," she assured Ella. "But that guy really didn't seem like Santa. He didn't like babies unless they were clean, and he didn't smile or say, 'Ho ho ho' a lot."

"Well, he was the best I could find," the photographer told Katie. "And now he's gone."

Katie blushed. She was really glad Ella and the photographer didn't know *that* was her fault, too.

"I could help you solve your problem," Katie volunteered.

"You?" Ella asked. "What could a kid like you do?"

"It's not like we have a kid-sized Santa costume here," the photographer told Katie.

"I don't need a costume," Katie assured him. "I just need a cell phone."

"A cell phone? Why?" the photographer asked.

"To call my grandmother," Katie explained. "She has a friend who would be perfect for the job!"

# Chapter 12

On Thursday morning, the kids in class 4A were practically bouncing out of their seats. They couldn't seem to learn a thing. All anyone could think about was the Secret Santa gift exchange.

Everyone really wanted to know who their Secret Santa was. And they couldn't wait to get their big gifts.

Everyone but Katie, that is. She wasn't looking forward to another gag gift. What would it be this time? Gum that tasted like pepper? A fake ice cube with a fly in it? Either way, it wasn't going to be something Katie liked. She was sure of it.

"Okay, you guys, I surrender," Mr. G. said. "I'm not going to be able to teach you kids anything until we exchange gifts. I'm going to be *impetuous* and let you go for it! Santas, deliver your presents!"

"Yeah!" George shouted as he leaped out of his beanbag chair. "I can't wait to see what I got!"

"Me, either," Kevin said. "I sure hope it's more tomato stuff."

Katie walked over to Kadeem and handed him her gift. "I'm your Secret Santa," she told him.

"Cool," Kadeem replied with a smile. "Those jokes really cracked me up."

"Then you'll really love this," Katie assured him.

Kadeem looked at the package. Once again there was a joke written on the wrapping. "Why did the girl pull the month off of her calendar?" he asked the class.

"Why?" Mandy Banks said.

"She wanted to take a month off!" Kadeem laughed. He opened his gift. "Check it out. A joke-a-day calendar!"

"That's three hundred and sixty-five jokes," Andrew said. "You could win lots of joke-offs with that!"

Katie watched as all her friends opened their presents. Andrew got an ant farm from George.

Kevin got a kit for growing tomatoes inside during the winter from Kadeem.

Mandy got a poster of her favorite Olympic ice-skater from Emma S.

George got a gift certificate to Louie's Pizza Shop from Mandy.

Emma W. got a diary and a pen from Kevin. Now that was a shock. Who knew that Kevin could buy nice gifts like a diary and a mood ring?

"My big brother Ian told me what to get," Kevin explained to Emma W. "He's in middle school. He knows all about what girls like."

Soon everyone had a gift from their Secret Santa. Everyone except Katie, that is.

Now Katie was really confused. Kadeem had been Kevin's Secret Santa. And George had been Andrew's. That meant the two biggest jokers in the class had not been giving her the gag gifts.

So who had?

Slowly, Emma W. walked over to Katie and handed her a package. It was soft and squishy, and it had a big red bow on top.

"You're my Secret Santa?" Katie asked, surprised.

Emma W. nodded.

"You gave me the fake vomit and the whoopee cushion?" Katie exclaimed.

"Uh-huh," Emma admitted. "I wanted to make sure you didn't know who your Secret Santa was."

"Well, it worked," Katie told her. "You were the last person I would have thought of."

"I know," Emma giggled. She looked at the

package in Katie's hands. "Aren't you going to open it?" she asked.

"I'm afraid to," Katie replied.

"Don't be. This is the real gift." Emma assured her.

Slowly, Katie untied the ribbon and opened the wrapping paper. Inside was a hat. It was made of fuzzy blue and white yarn. "It's beautiful!" Katie exclaimed.

"I knit it myself," Emma said proudly.

"You made this so fast!" Katie sounded really impressed.

"It's not that hard. I could teach you," Emma answered.

"That would be fun," Katie said as she placed the hat on her head.

"So, does the hat make up for the gag gifts?" Emma asked hopefully.

"Oh, yeah!" Katie replied. "This is the best Secret Santa ever!"

"Great." Emma sounded relieved. "Although I still think we should trick Mrs. Derkman into sitting on the whoopee cushion."

Katie giggled. "Now *that* would be some Christmas surprise!" she exclaimed.

# Chapter 13

That afternoon, Katie and her grandmother went to the mall together. Katie wore her new hat. Her grandmother wore a new hat, too. Hers was red and fuzzy with white trim.

"Come on, Katie, let's take a ride in that train!" her grandmother said as she paid for two tickets for the North Pole Express.

"You don't think it's babyish?" Katie asked her.

"No way," her grandmother said. She folded her legs up to her chin as she sat in the first car. The train was really meant for kids, so it was a very tight fit. "I'm pretending I'm on my way to the North Pole. I've always wanted to visit there."

"Me, too," Katie agreed. She climbed into the next car.

*Toot! Toot!* The train started around the track.

"You look just like Mrs. Claus in that hat," Katie told her grandmother.

"When you're in the North Pole, you have to dress the part." Her grandmother laughed. "Nick sure is!"

Katie looked over at Santa's chair. She knew the kids would love this Santa. His jelly

belly wasn't made by a pillow. His long white beard was real. And so was his laugh.

"Ho ho ho!" he chuckled loudly.

Katie grinned. Nick had the greatest laugh.

As the train came to a stop, Ella the Elf wandered over to Katie. "Hi, there," she said.

"Hi, Ella. This is my grandmother," Katie said.

"Your friend Nick makes a great Santa Claus," Ella told Katie's grandmother. "If I didn't know better, I would think he was the real thing."

"You're not the only one," Katie's grandmother chuckled. She pointed toward the front of the line.

Suzanne and Emma were standing there!

Katie walked right up to them. "Suzanne, I thought you said getting your picture taken with Santa was for babies."

Suzanne blushed. "Emma really wanted to come." Emma stared at Suzanne. "Okay, it was *my* idea," Suzanne admitted.

Katie giggled. "I get it. Why don't I get my picture taken with Santa, too? We could all do it together."

Suzanne smiled. "That would be fun."

When it was the girls' turn to visit Santa, Suzanne handed Nick a long list of gifts that she wanted. "Just in case," she whispered in his ear.

"Ho ho ho!" Nick laughed. "I'll see what I can do."

"Okay, everybody, say, 'Santa,'" the photographer shouted to the girls.

"SANTA!" the girls shouted back happily.

Katie grinned as the photographer snapped their picture. She really loved Santa. And *that* was no secret!